Young, Rich, Niggas

Thugs Need Love Too

Written by: Bianca Marie

This book is dedicated to my children, Ahmir and Alanna. I love you guys so much!! Everything I do, I do it for Y'all! You two inspire me to be great, and I promise I'm not gonna stop grinding until we get where we need to be. I love you, my babies!

A MESSAGE TO BIANCA'S BOMB ASS READERS!!!

I love you guys so much! I just wanna thank you guys for always rocking with me. Sometimes the journey is a rough one, but it's because of you guys that I keep pushing to keep producing some fire from my pen. I'm so happy that you guys enjoy everything I come with. I'm extremely grateful for my readers. I wouldn't be where I'm at today in this industry without the love from the readers. So, thank you!! I appreciate you all for rocking with me.

Xoxo_ Bianca Marie

<u>*WANT TO KNOW MORE ABOUT BIANCA MARIE?*</u>

Stay Updated Social Media handles

Add me on Facebook my main page @ Bianca Marie

Add my second Facebook page @ Authoress Bianca Marie

For sneak peeks, contests, and more join

my reader's group on Facebook @Bianca's Bookaholic's

Follow me on Instagram @ Biancamariebookz87

Follow me on Twitter @ BiancaBooks16

Prologue

GANGSTA

August 2012

"Let's go!" I shouted as I grabbed the bag with the money in it.

I threw the bag in the trunk of Lance's ride, and then me and my girl, Lanay, hopped in my Chevy Caprice. As I peeled

away from the pawn shop, my adrenaline rushed, and I felt on top of the world.

"Geon, baby! We did it! We fuckin' did it," Lanay shouted, and I laughed.

"Hell yeah, we did that shit." I felt good as I cruised on the highway. "Shit, my fucking hand!" Lanay looked at her hand, and I shook my

head. She was nervous as she cut the tape to place it on the workers' mouths, and she accidentally cut her hand with the box cutter.

"You was too nervous, bae." I chuckled

"Shit, I was, but I'm good, though. Do you think Lance is gonna be alright?" she asked me.

I looked over at her. Lance was my cousin who worked in the pawn shop. I shot him to make the scene look good.

"Yeah, he's gonna be good. It was only a flesh wound, bae. Stop tripping." I grinned.

This was the second joint I had robbed tonight, and I was a couple hundred thousand dollars richer.

Our euphoria was quickly dashed when blue and white lights flashed behind me, indicating for me to pull over.

"Oh shit," Lanay whispered.

"Just be cool, Ma, just be cool," I told her as I eased the car over to pull off the road.

When I did, two police officers stepped out of their cars with their guns drawn.

"Get the fuck outta the car!" they shouted, one on my side of the car, and the other on Lanay's side.

We both slowly stepped out of the car, and they threw me on the hood.

And then Lanay did something I thought she would never do.

"Oh My God! Please help me! He kidnapped me! He kidnapped me!" she screamed and cried buckets of tears.

The other officer looked at me with a scowl on his face. "Are you okay?" he asked her.

"No… I'm not," she cried and showing him her hand from when she accidentally cut herself while she was tying people up in the pawn shop;

"He… he cut me. Told me if I didn't listen, he would slice my throat next."

The whole time Lanay gave an Oscar worthy performance to the police officer, I was too in shock to even say shit. This bitch had just betrayed me like never before, and I knew I would never ever forget what that bitch just did.

The police escorted her to their vehicle, and she glanced back at me the mouthed the words, I'm sorry, like that shit was gonna make it any better. I was handcuffed and placed in the backseat of the police cruiser.

Chapter: 1 Geon "Gangsta" Rich

I'm a young fly nigga, I kick big shit, yeah Plus, my wrist lit, hey Plus, my bitch rich, yeah

I'm a big pimp, yeah I talk big shit, yeah

We got sticks bitch, yeah We don't miss shit, yeah uh

Yeah, wrist on frostbite, wedding bands look like headlights This the boss life, yeah

I rode down Chicago Avenue on the west side of Chicago bumping YFN Lucci and Offset's song, "Boss Life," because that's exactly what I was. A few minutes later, I pulled up to the stash house that me and my niggas operated out of.

I hopped out of my Benz and walked up on the porch. After I knocked three times on the window, the front door opened.

"My nigga, my nigga." Menace grinned when he saw me.

I dapped him up and went in the crib. Looking around, I saw that all my homies were in the building. Trill was sitting on the couch counting money out of the duffel bag from our last score.

"What's good with it, y'all?" I spoke.

"Shit but this money, nigga. Ya already know." Menace smiled.

That nigga loved some fucking money. That was his thing. I plopped in a chair that was next to the couch, and before

I could pull out my blunt, my cell phone rang. I pulled it outta my pocket and saw that it was my baby sister, Jasmine.

"What's up, sis?" I answered.

"G, Alan over here hitting Momma again," she whispered, and my nostrils flared in irritation.

"I'm on my way," I shouted then got up and headed for the door. "Where you going, nigga?" Menace asked me.

"That bitch ass nigga Alan, bruh," I responded while still walking out the front door.

"I'm riding with you," Menace announced and walked behind me. When I popped my locks, Trill got in the backseat.

That was why I fucked with them niggas. They ain't give a fuck; they were always down to ride for the muthafucking cause.

"What, y'all niggas thought y'all was gon' leave me?" Trill asked, and I chuckled.

I peeled away from the stash house and headed straight for my mom's crib. When I pulled up, Alan was outside showing his ass. He had my mother in the grass and beating her ass. My little sister, Jasmine, was standing in the doorway crying, and my younger sister, who was only nine years old, was screaming her fucking lungs out.

I was fucking heated. I hopped outta my ride then ran up and grabbed Alan by the back of his shirt, pulling him to the ground. Once he was down, I started beating the fuck outta his bitch ass. I was sick of the fuck nigga. Every time I tried to catch him, he somehow got away, but not this time.

Trill and Menace started beating the fucking brakes off him as well. All I could hear was my mom screaming at the top of her fucking lungs, telling us to stop.

"Geon, please… Geon…" my mom cried, but I ignored her.

I was out of breath as I kicked and stomped the shit outta

Alan. If my little sisters weren't there, I would've deaded this nigga on fucking sight. I was sick of his bitch ass.

"Geon... Geon..." he said my name through bloody, swollen lips, but I wasn't hearing that shit. He had fucked up for the last time with me.

"Bro, bro, please.... that's enough! That's enough!" Jasmine pleaded, grabbing my arm.

"Not in front of Leah," she begged me.

That was the only thing that calmed the beast in me.

I'm sorry, Geon, I'm sorry...." Alan's bitch ass cried out, but that shit was pointless because now he had to die.

I couldn't t let this nigga keep fucking breathing after this shit. I was done with it.

"Let's go, nigga," Trill snapped as we heard sirens getting closer.

I knew one of my mom's nosey ass neighbors had probably called the police as we were beating Alan's ass. I kicked him one last time in the fucking face and looked down at his ass.

"My name is Gangsta, bitch," I spat as I ran to my ride and hopped inside.

Me and my niggas sped off, and I couldn't help but crack a smile. I was sick and tired of the bitch ass nigga, and he got what the fuck he deserved. He wanted to keep beating on my moms, and she allowed it, but he wasn't gonna keep displaying that shit in front of my little sisters. I didn't give a fuck if Leah was his daughter. That was the only reason he wasn't dead right now. I didn't wanna kill my little sister's pops.

"Man, what's up with yo' OG? Why she keeps dealing with that goofy ass nigga?" Menace asked from the backseat.

I could smell the Kush he fired up and put in the air.

"Man, Ion know, but that weak ass nigga gotta go. I'm sick

and tired of his ass. He thinks my mom's a punching bag, and I'm not gonna keep allowing it," I snarled. I was more than pissed at my moms, though.

I had been out of jail for three years, and I had come up in life. Moving back to Chicago was the first thing I did when I got out. I tried to look for that bitch, Lanay, after she set me up, but I couldn't find her. That was cool too. I knew one of these days I would run back into her ass.

I was given six years the day I was locked up. Shit, my life had gone down the drain and fucking fast. Over the last three years, I had been building myself back the fuck up. I was taking no fucking prisoners. This Russian nigga gave me the name, Gangsta. Niggas tried me, and they failed each fucking time. I have a scar on my face from the first nigga who ever tried me in jail. Pussy ass nigga thought I was a bitch, and he learned the hard way who I really was.

I still had never fully forgiven my mother. She was supposed to be my rock. She was supposed to be there for me, but she wasn't. My mother gave me up the moment she saw trouble brewing. She claimed she couldn't take it. I was fourteen years old when she shipped me off to D.C. to live with my auntie Felicia and her three sons, my cousin Lance, Caleb, and Rinnie.

They lived in the heart of the projects called Simple City. Shit there was ten times worse than it was in Chicago. My moms sent my aunt money for me, but she never used it for me. Many nights I went hungry as fuck until I started robbing muthafuckas to just feed myself. Then, when I hit eighteen years old, I moved up in the robbing game. I started hitting pawn shops, liquor stores, and anything else that would put some money in my pocket. I was a bad seed, and there was nothing anyone could do to stop it.

I met the bitch, Lanay, while living in the projects, and she was everything to a young nigga. She was my first piece of pussy when I was fifteen years old, and she played me. Lanay was the first and last bitch I will give my heart to.

My mother was half Belizean, and my father was full blooded Belizean. I chose not to communicate with him as well. He was a sucker ass nigga who gave up his family and moved back to his country. My father was the man to see in his country. I didn't give a fuck how much clout a muthafucka had; he was a deadbeat, and I wanted nothing to do with him. He tried reaching out to me, but I was bitter. He called, and I never answered. He had messages delivered to me while I was in prison, and still I ignored all of his attempts.

Once I had gotten locked up, I became even more bitter. But then, I met my nigga, Kozlov. He was an older, Russian cat, and he was the one who gave me the name Gangsta. Kozlov gave me the game on this robbing shit, and now I refused to take a score less than 300,000. I had my bread stacked up, and I was a young nigga making moves now. Shit, I was a young, rich, nigga, and proud of how far I'd come in this game.

This day and age, I knew how to stake out art galleries for rare paintings, and when the shit closed, me and my niggas got in there and did what we did best. We sold them to the highest bidder, and that's where Kozlov came in. He was my connect with the art galleries and the powerful men in other countries who paid for those shits.

Art galleries, jewelry stores, and banks were me and my crew's thing. We staked them joints out, got the alarm system together, and were in and out under five minutes. It had been working for the last two and a half years, and we've seen more money than we could have ever imagined.

"Hell, yeah, fuck him," Trill added.

Menace and Trill were my niggas, but Trill was my dawg. He was the only nigga who had my back through it all. Me and Trill were more like brothers. Even when I moved to DC, me and that nigga stayed in touch. When I got locked up, he was the nigga putting money on my books, and when I got out, he was the one who picked me up, and we drove sixteen hours back to Chicago.

I didn't live with my moms when I came back to the Chi. It was his moms, Ms. Helen, who took me in and gave me a place to stay. And, for that, I would forever be grateful. I loved my mother, but I didn't view her as my moms. I viewed her as the lady who gave up on her only son. Still, I took care of her. I gave her and my sisters any and everything they wanted, but I fucked with her from a distance. I didn't visit, I didn't sit down with her and have dinner, I didn't take her shopping or no shit like that. I paid her bills and gave her a few dollars here and there, but no other special shit came from me.

I was bitter, and I wanted her to know just how bitter I was.

"Take me back to the spot, so I can finish counting up the money. Dre and the rest of them niggas in the spot, so I'm good," Trill said

"And what about you, Menace?"

"Take me to the crib. I gotta slide on Fallon," he said, and I nodded. "Nigga, I don't know how you deal with that gossiping ass bitch

Fallon." I sneered while shaking my head.

"Aye, Gangsta, watch ya fucking mouth talking about my bitch."

He got mad like he always did. Menace hated to hear the truth when it came to shit. He was the type of nigga who couldn't handle a joke, but shit, I wasn't joking. Fallon was a hoe.

"Man, whatever. I'm just saying, you acting like you ain't wifing a fucking hoe. That bitch Fallon done had so many dicks, I bet she know what the center of the lollipop looks like. Her ass..."

I started to go on, but I felt a punch in the back of my

head, and I damn near swerved off the fucking road.

"Nigga, what the fuck is wrong with you!" Trill shouted from the front seat while turning around to look at Menace.

I pulled over to the side of the road, and Menace hopped out.

"Bitch ass nigga, square up. I'm about to beat yo' ass," he snarled, and I just looked at his ass.

I wanted to get out of my ride and fuck him up, but we were brothers, and I wasn't built like that. I wasn't gonna put my hands on my homie. Once we went that route, it was no turning back, and I knew me. I wouldn't be able to fuck with him after that. So, to avoid all confrontation, I started my ignition and peeled away, leaving the trail of smoke in the air. I left his ass. If he thought we were about to fight because I was talking about that bitch, Fallon then, he had another thing coming.

"Nigga, you left him?" Trill laughed, and I glanced over and laughed too.

"Fuck Menace. That's what he gets for testing my Gangsta." I chuckled as I headed to drop Trill off.

∞

SITTING ACROSS FROM KOZLOV, I sipped my Hennessy as I listened to his proposition. I usually didn't meet with him without the guys, but he had a special assignment for me.

"You know I ain't into kidnapping muthafuckas," I spat, and he laughed heartily.

The old man still looked good for his age. He was the one who taught me the art of stealing. It was a finesse to everything you did in life, and that was something I took with me every day. He was released from prison shortly after me, and we connected right away. He sent his men to look for me.

"It's for a lot of money, Young Gangsta."

"I mean, I get it, but who is it?" I questioned.

He slid a picture over to me. The chick was fucking gorgeous. "And when I snatch her, what's next?" I asked.

"Kill her," he said with no remorse, and I didn't think twice about it. "Who the fuck she slump to get a hit out on her?" I was curious to

know as I took another sip from my drink.

"It's not her who's at fault. It's her boyfriend, a drug dealer who goes by the name Finesse." He slid his picture across to me, and I eyed it.

My jaws clenched in anger as I viewed the bitch nigga Finesse. I didn't know he had started going by that name, but me and this nigga had history. I touched the scar on the side of my face, and I got flashbacks from how I got it when I was in jail. It was all this nigga's fault. I didn't tell Kozlov that I knew who this nigga Finesse was, but I was determined to make this nigga and his bitch pay by any means.

After making sure everything I needed was in order, I got back on Kozlov's jet and flew back home. I had a new mission, and, as always, money was the fucking motive.

Chapter: 2 Aspen Walters

"That will be three sixty-five," I told Mayor Connelly.

He gave me the cash and an extra hundred dollars for a tip. I happily stuck the money in my bra.

Once the mayor left, I exhaled deeply. He was our last client for the night, and I was glad that the day was finally over.

"Girl, it was too damn busy today. What was it, lets cheat on my wife day today or some shit?" my sister, Aruba, said as she walked up to the front.

I looked at her and chuckled.

"Girl, I don't know what it was, but today we made some damn money," I exclaimed.

"Nah, Finesse made money," she replied with a roll of her eyes. "Don't do that, Ru, we did too!"

"Whatever, Aspen. I'm just calling it how I see it. That nigga is the one who rakes in all the cash while me, you, and Asia receive pennies. And let's not get on how much the girls make. Tuh, they're good because I would've been quit working here. It's not worth it"

"Will you shut the fuck up? What if one of them hears you?" I snapped at her hater ass.

Aruba got on my nerves at times with her crazy, talkative ass. She looked toward the back and shrugged.

"Look, I don't give a fuck. You need to tell ya man to stop being so damn cheap. The only reason I'm here is to help you. I swear I couldn't care fucking less about this shit," she snapped back.

I shook my head. I wasn't in the mood to have another debate with Aruba about this. It was her weekly routine, just full of fucking drama.

"Nah, you here because Finesse came through for you when…" I stopped mid-sentence when Asia came into the reception area.

"What the hell y'all arguing about now?" my little sister, Asia, asked. "What else? How I need to squeeze more money outta Finesse," I spat,

and Asia laughed.

"Ru, you still on that bullshit, huh?"

"What? Y'all bitches just hate me for my honesty. I'm just keeping it real."

"We know." Asia laughed. She walked over to the coat rack and grabbed her jacket.

"Where you going?" I inquired. I looked at the clock, and it was almost 10:00 at night.

"I have an exam that I have to study for. I can't be around you bitches all day and night. I'm not trying to work in a massage parlor for the rest of my life," she sarcastically spat, and I rolled my eyes.

"Bye, heffa. Call me when you get to your apartment. I mean it, Asia" "Okay, Mommy Dearest." She laughed as she walked out the front

door.

Me and Aruba sat around and waited until the girls were gone. Once they left, we got in our cars and went our separate ways.

As I drove, I couldn't stop thinking about what Asia said. I didn't wanna be stuck in the damn massage parlor for the rest of my life either. I wanted to bear some babies, make some real money, travel, and all that other shit, but I put all that on hold to be there for my man.

At twenty-five years old, I felt like an old ass woman, and that's not how it should've been. I had been with my nigga, Finesse, since I was a freshman in college. He was the typical dope boy, living the dope boy lifestyle, and I was infatuated with that. I was the perfect woman, if you ask me. Everything I did, I did for my nigga.

In the beginning, things were perfect. I felt like I was living a hood fairytale. Nothing Finesse could do was wrong in my eyes. I loved him so much, and I wanted to show him in every way possible how much he meant to me.

But, believe me when I say, Finesse didn't show how much he loved me. He was a hot fucking mess, and I wanted to change who he was so fucking badly, but I couldn't. He was gonna be him regardless. After all the things he put me through, I didn't understand how I could still be with him. Times when I should've walked away, I didn't, and I was the only one to blame.

I still loved him, but I didn't think that I was in love. I was with him out of convenience because he was comfortable. He took care of home as far as paying the bills and taking care of me, but buying me gifts and shit didn't make up for his lack of fidelity.

When I pulled into the driveway of our million-dollar home, I exhaled deeply. I didn't see Finesse 's car in the driveway, and I knew that must've meant one thing. He was out in the streets with her. Finesse had some broad that he was smashing on the regular, but I refused to let this random ass bitch win. Fuck that. I was first, and I would be his last.

I got out of my car and went inside to get ready for another night without my man. As soon as I entered the crib, I stripped outta my clothing and hopped in the shower. It was something about cascading hot ass water hitting my backside. The shit felt like such a stress relief.

Thinking about my sisters and where we are today, coming from a two-parent home, one wouldn't have imagined we would live our lives the way that we did. It was the typical church daddy and first lady bullshit with three wild ass daughters. My father was a preacher. Denver Walters was the pastor of First Christ Baptist church. My father had the biggest church congregation on the east side of Chicago.

My daddy was as strict as they came, and when me and my sisters saw our way out, we were on the first thing smoking outta their house. I was the one who endured the most scrutiny. I went to college to pursue a career in social work, but that was a fail once I met Finesse. He took up the majority of my time, and I quit college. I only had myself to blame because I allowed him to take everything from me.

After showering, I put on some boy shorts and a cami. I looked myself over in the mirror, and I was amazed by what I saw. And y'all know what I saw? I saw nothing; a girl with no hope, no ambition, no drive. I let a man be my everything when I wasn't his everything. And in the end, he brought me down to the lowest of the low.

I ended up dozing off to sleep and was awakened by kisses on the forehead. Finesse had come into the bedroom. I sat up and looked at him. Even after all these years, he was still as fine as the day I met him. long dreadlocks that touched the middle of his back, peanut butter skin complexion, and a smile to make any girl's panties wet.

"What's good, bae?" Finesse said to me. "Hey." I yawned

"How was your day?" he asked as he took off his shirt. I couldn't help but look at his chiseled chest.

"It was cool. Long and tiring as usual. What about you? How was your day?" I asked.

"It was cool. Out trapping, checking niggas, the norm." He chuckled then tossed his phone, money, and keys on the nightstand before he walked into the bathroom.

My eyes scanned the contents that were lying on the nightstand. I contemplated going in his phone. I mean, I was a woman, and I knew my nigga was unfaithful to me, so why would I even look? Well, that answer was simple; I was a woman.

I grabbed the phone off the nightstand, and before I could even peek into it, it started to ring. Agitation filled my face when I saw the name pop up on the screen. This nigga was as bold as they came. Girlfriend #2. I didn't know if he called himself being funny, but I didn't see the joke in it. I usually didn't pop shit with Finesse; he was the man, so I felt that there was no need for me to be aggressive or anything like that, but I now understood that's why he disrespected me. Instead of my not saying anything, I answered it.,

"Hello?" I spoke into the phone, and the chick on the other end was quiet as hell.

"Hello?" I shouted again

"Where's Finesse?" she asked, and I chuckled. She was bold as fuck "He's asleep. Who is this?"'

"You know who I am, Aspen," she said, and I pulled the phone away from my face. She was bold as fuck as she said that shit. The fuck did she mean I knew who she was? I was startled, so I didn't have a comeback for her ass

"Cat got cha tongue, bitch?" she cackled, and I frowned.

"Yeah, I know who you are, just like you know who I am. And you know side chick hours are over, bitch. He's at home with his woman. So, get the fuck off this line and don't call back no more," I snapped and hung up the phone in her face.

Finesse came out the bathroom, and he had a confused look on his face.

"Who were you talking to?" he asked me.

I didn't respond. I only looked at his disrespectful ass.

"Who the fuck were you talking to?" he barked, and I shook my head. "You know who, Finesse. Ya bitch, ya mistress, side chick, or

whatever you wanna call her," I snapped back.

"Yoooo, why the fuck are you answering my phone?" I couldn't believe that was all he had to say.

"Whatchu mean? I can answer yo' shit. Don't you answer mine?" I snapped back at him.

"Still, that could've been business."

"Who is she, Finesse?"

"None of ya fucking business. That's ya fucking problem. Always worried about the wrong shit. And you wonder why I ain't married ya dumb ass yet," he growled, and I threw a pillow at his ass.

"Fuck you! You ain't married me yet because you a piece of shit," I shouted.

"Man, you know what.... fuck this! I ain't about to argue with yo dumb ass," he said in a low tone and grabbed his shirt then put it over his head.

My heart rate increased because he was about to walk out the door again.

"Whatchu doing?" I asked as I hopped off the bed and walked up on him.

I grabbed him back by his shirt, but he snatched away from me.

"Man, get the fuck off of me," he growled and turned around to face me.

I slapped the shit out of him. He looked at me and then he slapped me

back. I fell to the floor, but I refused to cry. I was sick of his disrespectful ass.

"Don't put ya fucking hands on me, Aspen! What type of nigga you take me for?" he shouted.

"Finesse…" I whispered his name.

"Nah, I'm out bitch. Until you learn some muthafucking respect, I won't be back," he argued, and I couldn't believe my ears.

"If you walk out that door, I won't be here when you get back," I threatened, and he only chuckled.

"Do you, shawty, cuz I'm out," he snapped and walked out of the bedroom.

I was disgusted with my situation, and I didn't know what to say or what to do. Running home to my parents wasn't an option because they would know I had failed miserably at this shit. Tears fell from my eyes. I was sick and tired of Finesse 's ass. If only I didn't love this nigga as much as did. Lord knows I would've been left him. I was just dumb. And I knew for a fact that he was going to run back into the arms of whoever the side chick was.

Once I heard the front door slam, I broke down to my knees and prayed to God for strength to help me leave this nigga.

Chapter: 3 Trill

"Damn, shawty, you suck a nigga dick like that again, I'm gon' fuck around and wife ya ass up." I chuckled as I headed for the bathroom.

I was kicking it was this lil shawty by the name of Nika, and she was good as fuck at sucking a nigga off. As much as I liked the head, I didn't like her. She was a thot out here fucking all types of niggas. I was lying when I said I was gonna wife her ass up. Not! I didn't give a fuck about none of these hoes. If it didn't make dollars, it didn't make sense.

"You coming back over here later?" she came and stood in the bathroom doorway

"Nah, I'm not," I told her honestly.

Shit, I wasn't about to lie to her ass. That wouldn't be me. I had to pick my little brother up from school in a little while, and I couldn't be fooling around with this emotional ass bitch.

"Well, that was easy for you, huh?" she sarcastically spat

"Yeah, it was, shawty." I chuckled as I buttoned my pants and walked out of her front door.

I hopped in my ride and peeled away from her spot, tossing her to the back of my mind like I did the rest of these bitches.

My cell chimed, and it was this nigga Menace calling me. I chuckled when I saw his name on my screen.

"Whaddup, nigga?"

"Nigga, fuck you," he snapped, and I laughed.

"Ain't shit funny, bro. G left me like that. That nigga is foul, and I ain't fucking with him no more," he argued, and I continued to laugh. The shit was hilarious to me.

Gangsta was always so serious, and Menace was always so fucking sensitive. I guess I was the fucking balance.

"Nah, nigga, you fucked that up! You tried to fight the mans over some shit you know is the fucking truth, bruh," I told him.

That bitch, Fallon, was a fucking hoe, and he just needed to face the fact.

"Man, fuck all of that. Y'all niggas don't know what y'all spitting. My shorty is faithful to me. That's why I'm marrying her," he said, and I shook my head.

This nigga was always head over heels in love with these bitches. If he married, Fallon, he was about to be the dumbest nigga in the fucking world.

"Man, ya ass a goofy, but that's yo life and funeral," I joked.

"Nigga, you still gonna be my best man though, right?" he asked, and that made me burst into laughter.

"Nigga, I gotchu." I chuckled

"So, what's up? When we making this move?" he asked.

"We gotta me at the spot tonight at eight. G wanna go over some last-minute details."

"This nigga and this last-minute shit," he scoffed, complaining as usual.

"Yo, nigga, get the fuck off my line sounding like a bitch. I just pulled up in front of my mom's crib. I'll hit you back," I said and hung up the phone before he could even respond.

Menace was a fucking headache, but that was my nigga,

though. Him and Gangsta always got into arguments and fights, but it wasn't shit that would ever stop us from being homies. Those were my niggas to the death of me. I loved both like my moms birthed them as well.

Me and my homies were some young, rich, fly ass niggas. We were what you called the robbers. Basically, we took every fucking thing. We didn't fuck with drug dealers and shit because that was small shit. We hit big ass banks, jewelry stores, galleries, all type of shit.

With one job, we usually walked out of the bank with about 750,000. We killed guards and one worker just to keep everybody on their toes. Once they saw we were not playing, they moved fast as fuck. We be low key, so the FBI wouldn't get on our trail. We'd been doing this robbing shit for about three years, and the money was lovely.

I'm not gonna lie and say me and my niggas keep a low profile because we don't. We fuck off the money, hit strip clubs, and buy jewelry. All that shit. Some might say we were dumb, or better yet, cocky, but we hadn't been caught yet, and I didn't think we would ever get caught.

Gangsta was good at casing the banks out, and he always made sure shit ran smoothly as possible. Gangsta didn't have a problem murking niggas, but I was a little bit sicker in the head than him. He was reasonable while I gave no fucks at all.

I pulled up to Loyola University to pick my little brother, Rico, up for the weekend. He stayed on their campus for the dumbest reason when he could've been right at the crib with me and my moms. I sparked up a blunt as I watched the thick ass chicks float by my whip. They had their bookbags attached to their backs, and they were moving fast as hell.

One shorty captured my attention, though. She was dark-skinned, and that ass was fat than a muthafucka. But it wasn't the ass that held my attention, it was her smile. Her teeth were white as fuck against her chocolate ass skin. She was engrossed in her phone conversation, so I decided to fuck with her. I honked my horn, and she jumped and looked my way.

"Damn, stupid ass," she snapped, and I chuckled.

She was mean mugging the fuck outta me, but she couldn't see who I was due to the tint on my windows. I let my window down before she could fully get away.

"What the fuck was that smart shit you just said outta ya mouth?" I grinned, and she looked at me and rolled her eyes.

"Nigga, fuck you," she shouted, and I cracked up laughing.

Rico was casually strolling my way when he and shorty stopped and started chatting. She hugged him, and he walked to my whip. Now, I was more than curious to get to know who shawty was. I hoped lil bro wasn't smashing because that shit would've put a damper on my plans.

Rico hopped in my ride and grinned. "What's good, broski?" he dapped me up.

"Shit, my nigga. What's up? You ready?" I asked. He nodded, and I started my ignition then peeled off.

"Who was shawty you were just hugging?" I had to ask as I merged into traffic on Lake Shore Drive.

"Who, Asia?" he questioned.

"Nigga, Ion know her fucking name. You smashing that?"

He laughed. "Nah, that's my homie. We in a study group together." "Your fa sho' about that?" I asked with a raised eyebrow.

"I'm positive, goofy," he said and laughed.

Goofy was something we called each other when we were fucking around. I started to respond, but his phone rang.

"Speaking of Asia, this is her right now," he said and showed me his phone.

I smirked as he answered.

"Yeah, hold on, sis," he stated, and then I noticed he put his phone on speaker.

"You on speaker, sis. Say whatchu need to say." He laughed. Her soft ass voice boomed through the speaker, and I chuckled.

"Nigga, the next time you wanna holla at someone, don't honk ya fucking horn at me. You cute and all, but that ain't the way to go about it," she spoke.

"Is that right?" I responded.

"Yeah, that's right. You're lucky Rico is my homie, or I would've cursed you the fuck out," she snapped, and I laughed again.

"Well, any homie of Rico's is my homie. Can we be homies, Ms.

Asia?" I asked.

"Rico, you told him my name!" she squealed, and we both started laughing.

'That's my big brother, A... my bad, my bad."

"It's all good, but look, I don't know, Mr. Let Me Honk My Horn at Someone."

"Well, think about it, and I'll find out tonight when I come and pick you up," I told her.

"You don't even have my address, with ya cocky ass. Matter of fact, I don't even know your name," she said, slightly agitated.

"My name is Rahmeek, but the streets call me Trill... You can call me either one, but I would prefer daddy," I told her, and Rico burst into laughter.

"Nah, nigga, I got a daddy who's still married to my momma... But, yeah, get my number from Rico, and maybe, just maybe I'll take you up on your offer for a date. I'm heading into class now. Bye, Trill, and bye Rico," she said and hung the phone.

"Nigga, yo ass is wild." Rico laughed.

"Man, I'm gon' have that ass wide the fuck open, with her sexy ass." I chuckled as I thought about Asia being another one added to my long list of hoes.

THREE DAYS LATER, I pulled up in front of Asia's crib at 8:30. She was already sitting on her front porch. My window was down, so I could smell the weed she had fired up and put in the air. That shit smelled like it was some fire.

"You ready?" I hollered, and she just stared at me.

She didn't get off the porch to come and get in the car, nor did she open her mouth. She only stared at me.

"You ain't gon' move or say nothing, shawty?" I asked.

What the fuck was she on? I hoped this bitch didn't waste my time. I had a million thoughts running through my head, trying to figure her ass out.

"Nigga, you ain't gon' get out the car and open the door?" she asked.

I laughed. So that's what she wanted? I wasn't used to giving the gentleman treatment to these bitches. I hopped out my ride and opened the door for her. She got off the porch and walked toward me. I took in her appearance, and she was fly ass fuck. Her bob length hair was curled, her lips, which were big and plump had some glittery shit on it that made them muthafuckas look delectable, and she was sporting a tight ass yellow dress that hugged every curve on her body. She wasn't a super small framed chick, but she wasn't big either. She had a small pudge in her tummy, but that shit didn't bother me at all. I liked what I saw.

She got in my ride, and I closed the door. Then I ran around to the driver side door and hopped inside.

"What's good, shawty?" I glanced over at her.

"Shit. What's up with ya cocky, arrogant ass?" She sneered, and I laughed at her.

I started my ignition and peeled away.

"Now, what makes you think I'm so cocky? You don't even know me yet."

"Your whole demeanor states that you're cocky. You think because you got a nice ride, some jewelry around ya neck, and a lil money that you just got this shit."

"I ain't got a lil money, I got a whole lot of money, shawty," I said, and she rolled her eyes.

"See what I mean? Cocky shit," she spat, causing me to laugh.

"Nah, I ain't cocky, and if I'm so cocky, you sholl sitting ya chocolate, thick ass right here," I told her.

"I am because I'm probably dumb ass as hell for sitting here. At the same time, I'm young, so I'm taking a risk like young bitches do," she admitted, and I cracked the fuck up.

"Yoooo, shorty, you funny as fuck." "Whatever, nigga." She scoffed.

"Where we going?"

"I don't know. I don't do dates and shit," I confessed. "Then what the fuck do you do?" she questioned. "Fuck," I spat, and she shook her head.

"Well, I don't want no fucking food, so let's go have drinks. It's this dope ass spot called The Island Bar, and they be having some banging ass wings. It's a sports bar, but it's pretty laid back," she suggested.

I already knew the spot because we robbed the joint

in the beginning of our robbing career. That was considered chump change to us now.

"Aight, bet." I headed in the direction of the sports bar, and me and Asia continued small talk.

I liked her swag. She was also smart as fuck. Her intellect shined through that tough girl persona. I could tell she was educated, and I loved that shit on a black woman. My mom was smart as fuck. She'd been in school damn near me and Rico's whole life. That's how I basically got into the street life. My moms was so busy going to school and working that she couldn't be at home with us like she wanted. I knew she wanted better for me, but the streets were my calling.

Rico was gonna be the one to make something of himself. I was just a street nigga waiting for my expiration date. At twenty-four years old, I had never been in love and didn't plan on it. I didn't have kids, no maybe babies, none of that shit. I was always a careful nigga, unlike Menace, who stayed falling in love with a bitch. I just couldn't do it. I had seen the most loyal bitches set up niggas who they claimed to love so much for a couple of bands. Pussy will make you lose your life, and I refused to be a victim of the shit.

Once we made it to the bar, we grabbed a table, and I ordered our drinks. Asia was the typical chick. She wanted a damn long island iced tea. I got a henny on the rocks.

"So, whatchu going to school for, Ms. Asia?" I asked. I stared into her pretty ass eyes, and she smiled.

"Criminal Justice and politics," she stated, and my eyes widened. Most bitches said psychology or social work.

"Oh, wow. That's dope, ma."

"Yeah, yeah. I know. It's tiring, though."

"So, you smoking weed and shit? They not gon' penalize you for that?" I asked, and she laughed.

"Nigga, I still go to school. I gotta attend law school and some more shit before I get a job, so I'm good until then."

"How about that? I'm on a date with my future defense attorney, 'cause a nigga like me just might be locked up one of these days," I joked. "Well, I think all the weed will be outta my system by then, so I can

properly represent you." She chuckled. "True, true."

"So, what is it that you do, Trill?"

"I'm a freelancer," I stated, and she laughed loudly. "I like that."

"Shit, me too." We both chuckled.

"How old are you, Ms. Asia? What's ya family like?"

"I'm twenty-two, I'll be twenty-three in May. I have two sisters, and my mother and father are still married. I'm the baby of the family, and no, I'm not spoiled." She smirked.

"I can tell that was a lie... the part about not being spoiled," I said, and she pushed me.

"Whatever... so is Rico your only sibling?" "Yup, just me and lil bro." I nodded.

She started to say something else, but the waitress walked over with the hot wings and placed them in front of us before she handed us both our drinks.

We dug in and slammed the hot wings. By the time the night was winding down, I was a little tipsy. We were sitting in a booth, and Asia cozied up next to me. I put my arm around her shoulder, and I liked the way her hair smelled.

"Whatchu got on?" I whispered in a husky voice. She was smelling good as shit.

"Oh, that's Nude by Rhianna. I love it. It's one of my favorite perfumes," she said.

"That shit is making my dick hard," I spoke honestly, and

she chuckled.

I hated when I got drunk. Anything was liable to come out my mouth, and that's exactly what happened.

"Yeah?" she questioned then laughed.

"I'm gonna start calling you Lips, 'cause them muthafuckas plump and juicy as shit," I told her, and she grinned.

"Lips, huh?" "Hell yeah."

"You wanna see what these lips can do?" she whispered. "Hell yeah."

Then she did something I didn't expect. She leaned over, gently kissed the side of my neck, then took her right hand and placed it in my Nike joggers. She found my dick. Thank God the table was covering her actions, but the touch of her warm hand on my dick caused him to jerk a little. Shit, I was drunk and fucking horny. She better stop playing with me before I fucked her in front of all these muthafuckas.

She slowly stroked my dick. I had to close my eyes to keep my composure because the shit felt good as fuck. I looked down at her, and she was looking up at me.

"Whatchu looking at?" I asked. "You." She grinned.

"Whatchu looking at me for?"

"You like that shit, don't you?" she asked.

"Hell yeah. I wanna fuck you so bad right now." "I know... I know," she said and sped up her pace.

If she thought I was gonna bust from her hand job, she me fucked up. I was saving all this nut for her throat.

"Aye, let's go," I demanded.

She removed her hand, and I adjusted my dick before getting out of the booth. I threw a couple of hundreds on the table, and we walked out of the bar. When we got to the parking lot,

I popped the locks and told her ass to get in my ride. I glanced over at her, and she smirked.

"What, nigga?" She laughed.

"Lemme find out college girl is a freak," I said.

"I am, but only with who I wanna be freaky with."

"Mmmhmmm, you ready for me to make that pussy sing?" I eyed her. "Nigga, who said I was fucking you?" she questioned, and I instantly

frowned.

Now this bitch wanted to play games. I wasn't about to play with her, and my dick was rock hard. I needed pussy, and now. Nah, before I got mad, I decided to drop this bitch off. I didn't say another word as I started my ignition and peeled off, heading to her house.

The entire drive, it was quiet in the car, and I could feel her looking at

me.

"You mad or something, Trill?" she asked.

"Nah, I'm good, shawty. I don't get mad. I get me another one.

Simple."

She laughed. "I hate seeing niggas so pressed, my God," she spoke.

I exhaled deeply. Asia was a mess, and I'd be damned if she took me out of character tonight. When I pulled up to her crib, she just sat there. What the fuck was she waiting for?

"Can I get a kiss goodnight?" She smiled, and I shook my head.

"Yo, what the fuck is you on?" I asked. This bitch was playing games. "I asked for a good night kiss. Just one, Trill, damn." She said my

name like we'd been lovers forever or some shit.

"Can my dick have a kiss? Fuck you mean. Lips, stop playing with me, aight?"

She laughed again like some shit was funny.

"Nigga, shut the fuck up," she spat and then leaned up and kissed my lips.

I couldn't do anything because once I felt them muthafuckas touch my lips, I knew I was gonna kiss her ass back. She slipped her tongue in my mouth and gently bit my bottom lip, causing my dick to get hard all over again. Then, she slid in my seat and straddled me cowgirl style. We never broke our kiss as she leaned up some, and I pulled the spaghetti straps down, revealing her chocolate ass nipples.

I placed one of them in my mouth and gently sucked on it. She threw her head back in pleasure then removed my dick from my joggers and began to slowly stroke him. She played with the pre-cum on the tip of my dick. I was tired of playing cat and mouse with her ass, so I grabbed a condom out of my glove compartment and placed it on my dick.

I instructed her to sit up for a second. After she did that, she sat back down on my dick. Her warmth had my shit feeling nice. She started to grind, rock, and bounce gently on my dick. She had some skills with riding because most bitches didn't know how to ride dick. If you could ride dick and don't get tired, you were a keeper in my book.

"Ahhhhhh, fuck," I hissed as I looked into her eyes.

She was smiling like she was doing some shit, which she was, but her tone switched up when I started bucking her back.

"Ohhhhhhh, shit! Baby!" she screamed.

We were fucking right in front of her parents' crib. Shit was odd as hell to me, but at the same time, I didn't give a fuck.

"Yeah, bounce that pussy, baby." I groaned as I squeezed her nipples and played with them.

"Ohhhhhhh, Trill. Shit feels so good."

She was right because I felt like her pussy was heaven. She was wet as fuck, and I loved that shit. I grabbed her by the back of her head and leaned her toward me. I kissed her roughly as I fucked her back. Her pussy gripped my dick tighter and tighter, and I knew she was about to cum. I leaned her back while she was still riding, and her back started pressing the horn. The lights in her parents' house came on after the horn blast, but neither of us cared. I played with her clit, and she went crazy.

"Ohhhhhhh shit! Ohhhhhhh Baby! Yesssssss Dadddddyy-yyy Yesssssss Daddy I'm about to cummmmm!" she screamed and squirted all over my dick.

While she was trying to catch her breath, I never stopped fucking her. Instead, I went even harder. Hearing her say that daddy shit did something to me, and within seconds, I came right behind her.

We were both panting and out of breath. She slid back over in her seat, looked at me, and laughed.

"That was some good dick right there." She adjusted her dress as I took the condom off my dick and threw it out of the car.

"That's some good pussy," I told her with a smirk. "I know," she stated and opened the car door. "Who's the cocky one now?" I hollered behind her.

"Good night, Rahmeek," she said, and I smiled at hearing her call me by my first name.

I started my ignition, and before I peeled off, I hollered out the window. "Aye, Lips!"

She turned around and looked at me.

"I told you, you was gonna call me daddy!"

She stuck her middle finger up, and I laughed as I peeled off and headed home.

Chapter 4: Asia Walters

"Good morning, sleepy head," my mother said as I walked into the kitchen.

I let out a yawn as I scratched my head. I was dead ass tired from fucking around with Trill last night.

"Morning, Ma." I kissed her on the cheek and sat down next to her at the table.

I usually stayed at my off-campus apartment, but I was too tired to drive back last night.

"Have you spoken to your sisters?" she asked me as she sipped her coffee.

"Nah, I'm about to go up to the job in a few minutes," I said.

"How was your morning?" I asked as I poured myself some orange juice.

"It's fine, just waiting for your father to come back home. How has school been going?"

"It's fine. The classes are getting harder and harder. You know how that goes." I shrugged.

"Well, I'm very proud of you, sweetheart. At least you stuck with it, unlike Aspen and Aruba, who didn't care to do anything with their lives." She grunted, and I shook my head. I hated when she talked about my sisters.

"They are doing something with their lives," I shot back. "Like what?" She laughed and sipped her coffee again. "Like working. Most females ain't even out here working."

"They're working in a massage parlor for Aspen's drug dealer boyfriend. If you call that doing something with your life, then I don't know what to say."

"Momma, that's just wrong now. You don't work and never have. You were comfortable being Daddy's everything," I told her, and her eyes widened.

"Don't you dare disrespect me in that way. I'm your mother! All my life I've taken care of you girls. I've made everything about you! Never once in my life since I had children did I ever make anything about myself."

She was offended, but Aspen was a lot like her when it came to a man. She did whatever for my father, and she never went against his word. She never took up for us; anything Daddy wanted, anything Daddy asked for was Halle's command.

"I'm sorry if you feel I disrespected you, Mom." I got up from the kitchen table and kissed her cheek.

"Is this why Aspen doesn't come home? Is this why she doesn't call or answer my phone calls?" she asked, and I exhaled deeply.

"Momma, I don't know why Aspen doesn't come around," I replied, and I continued to walk away.

I knew it was my best bet to walk away because I was very blunt, and I didn't bite my tongue. If I wanted to say it, then I was gonna say it. And I would probably hurt my mom's feelings when I gave her the real. She knew how I was. I wasn't gonna sugarcoat shit. On top of that, Aspen had been bitter about my parents for a long time, but she's never expressed to us why she felt the way she did. So, I couldn't answer her question even if I wanted to.

I didn't even shower. Instead, I grabbed my shit and left

their house. I wasn't in the mood to be dealing with her and my father anyway, so I was gonna head into the massage parlor, but I was dead ass tired. At the last minute, I decided to go home and get some more rest instead of into work. I was taking my own day off. Fuck it.

∞

THIS MORNING, I felt revived, so I showered, got dressed, and then hopped in my ride and headed to the massage parlor. Aspen had been calling me all fucking morning, and I refused to answer. I knew it was because I didn't come in to work yesterday. She thought she was my mother at times, and I had to remind her time and time again that she wasn't my momma.

When I made it in the massage parlor, Aspen was behind the counter.

She looked up at me with blood shot red eyes. I could tell she had been crying. Probably about some shit Finesse lame ass did to her. I couldn't stand the nigga, but he paid good, and this money was helping me while I was in school.

"What's wrong with you?" I asked.

"Nothing, I'm good, but what's up with you? Where you been?" she asked me.

"Girl, at home. I was tired as shit yesterday." "Oh, what hell were you doing?" She eyed me

"I went out on a date the other night." I smiled thinking about Trill's big dick ass.

"Oh, really now?" She smirked "Girl, yeah, and he was so dope…"

I couldn't finish my sentence because the front door opened, and Aruba walked through looking mean as hell. Oh lord, I thought.

"Who the fuck is in my parking space, Aspen?" she snapped, and I just stared at her dramatic ass.

"Ru, I don't know. Shit, probably a customer," Aspen responded. "Well, y'all need to put a sign out there that this space is taken. The

fuck. I had to park all the way around the back of the place. Y'all must be making some money today, huh?" She frowned.

My sister was gorgeous; she was just mean as hell, dramatic, and childish at times.

"Girllllllllll, shut the fuck up! Always whining and shit," I snapped, and Aspen laughed.

"That mouth shouldn't be used for a future lawyer," Ru stated.

I ignored her and headed to the back where the supply closet was located. Once inside, I sat on the stool. This was my hideaway spot. Aspen didn't know that I really didn't do any fucking work. I pulled out my phone and scrolled Instagram and Facebook as I waited for the hours to pass.

I heard voices, and the male voice was all too familiar. I opened the supply closet and spotted one of the workers holding Professor Garrett's hand. My eyes widened, and I couldn't believe what I saw. My fucking professor. He looked toward the closet, and I hurriedly slammed the door.

"What the fuck?" I whispered.

He was the same muthafucka talking about failing me, and here he was getting a happy ending at the end of his massage. Lousy muthafucka.

I sat in the closet for about an hour with my mind going in circles, trying to figure out why the fuck Professor Garrett was there. I exited the closet, and when I walked back to the front, I spotted the back of his head leaving out the door. He didn't even look back and notice me.

"What's up, sis? You okay?" Aspen's cheery ass asked me "Yeah, I'm good. When does dude come back who just left?" I had devised a plan in mind, and I needed it to work.

"Oh, Garrett? He usually comes on Mondays, so it's a shocker that he's here today."

Mondays, that's why I never saw him. He came when he didn't have classes, and that was the day I had the longest classes. Although I didn't have his class on Monday, I still was in school for damn near eight hours, so I didn't come to the massage parlor on Mondays and Wednesdays.

"Oh, okay."

"Why you asking about Garrett?" Aspen's nosey ass asked. "He looks like a big tipper," I played it off.

"Oh, that he is."

"Yeah, I'm gonna hop on that the next time he comes." "You'll be in school, Asia."

"Nah, I'm gonna make sure I'm here. I need all the money I can get." I let another lie roll off my tongue.

Professor Garrett was a thorn in my ass, and I couldn't wait to knock him down a notch.

I finished up at the parlor with my sisters, and then I headed home. Once home, I hopped in the shower, and Trill's sexy face ran across my mind. He was light skinned with tats all over his body and a slender build, but he wasn't skinny. The muscles he did have were sexy as fuck.

I was pissed that he hadn't called me yet after I gave him my goodies, but I knew that was how niggas operated. He was a street nigga, straight to the code ass nigga. The dick was good while it lasted, but I wasn't gonna stalk his ass, even if I was feeling some type of way. Shit, I was in college. Spontaneous sex was my thing any fucking way.

After showering, I lay across my bed and turned on the television. Reruns of Law and Order SVU were on. It was almost midnight, and I surprised the shit was still on. My cell chimed, and it was a text message from Aruba.

Ru: Wyd?

Me: Shit, in bed. What's up?

Ru: Let's go out for a drink. Meechie just pissed me off!

Me: Lmao! Give me twenty minutes and text me where you wanna meet.

After texting Ru back, I got up and got dressed. I pulled out my army fatigue one-piece jumper and my black, thigh high boots. My bob still looked good, so I took my curlers and threw some wild curls in it then fluffed it real good. Once I had on my leather jacket and gold, hoop earrings, I was out the door. I was never one of those chicks who took forever and a day to get ready.

After receiving the text message from Ru on where she wanted to go, I hopped in my ride and headed to The Dynasty. It was a dope ass bar that sold these frozen ass drinks like you were at Wet Willy's in Miami. It was always live, and it was a Saturday, so I knew it was popping.

Making it to the club, I found Aruba's car. I hopped out and walked over to her ride. She got of the car and my eyes widened at how she was dressed.

"Damn, bitch, you tryna get yo hoe hoe on tonight, huh?" I laughed, and she smiled.

"What? You think it's too much?" she questioned. "Hell naw, bitch... You know I love that type of shit."

I grinned. Aruba was sporting a tight ass black dress, her short, black mink jacket, and some black six inch stilettos. Her hair was in a bun, and her makeup was done to perfection. Sis was gorgeous as fuck.

"I know you do, slut." She giggled, and I grabbed her hand. We walked to the club entry doors, and who do we see at the fucking door? I could strangle her ass for this one. Her dude, Meechie, was the bouncer at the club.

When he saw us, he smirked.

"Y'all ain't getting in this muthafucka," Meechie growled staring at Ru's attire.

She had a smile on her face, and I was pissed. I didn't come out all dressed up to play no fucking games with her and her nigga.

"Meechie, stop playing with me," Ru said.

"Come on. Move the line, damn!" a girl behind us said. I turned around and mugged the bitch.

"Aye, Meechie, come on, man. I ain't got time for this shit." I exhaled. "Like I said, no fucking entry. Take ya ass home, Ru," he snapped. "Hol up! Muthafucka, you got us…"

I stopped midsentence when a group of niggas got everybody's attention. They were flashy as fuck, big ass iced out chains, glistening ass watches, and Gucci shades on their faces. Bitches were speaking and drooling over them as if they were some celebrities or some shit.

"Whaddup, Gangsta?" Meechie spoke to the big nigga who was ahead of the crowd.

Meechie allowed them in with no problem. It was about ten of them niggas, and that only pissed me off more.

"Really, Meechie!" I shrieked as the last nigga was came through the door.

We locked eyes. It was Trill. He looked good as fuck with some dark ass shades on his face, dressed in all black, and the jewels he was rocking were the truth. Damn, he looked good. He looked me over and smirked. I couldn't help but let a smile form on my face.

"They with us, Meechie," he said, and Meechie frowned.

He didn't wanna let Aruba in the club, and he knew it was because she could find better than his lame ass. He allowed us to enter. Once inside, I looked at Trill and smiled.

"Thanks," I said, then grabbed Ru's hand and led her away from him. I didn't want the nigga to think I was pressed.

"Bitch, who the fuck is that?" she asked me once we made it to the bar. "A nigga I fucked two days ago," I boldly stated, and her eyes

widened.

"Bitch, what?"

"Yeah, and the dick was good too, but fuck him. Let's turn the fuck up," I screeched.

I ordered a long island from the bar and Ru a Patron margarita. We got tipsy, talked shit, and flirted with the many guys who approached us.

My song blared through the speakers, and I knew it was time to shake my ass.

I tell him eat the cookie 'cause it's good for him And when he eat the cookie he got good form

He know I don't ever cheat because I'm good to him Might gotta have his baby, nurses yellin' push for him You see I let him eat the cookie 'cause it's good for him And when he bite, he eat the cookie he got good form He know that when I'm pullin' up I'm in a good foreign I be like ooh he love me, ooh he love me, good form

Nicki Minaj's "Good Form" blared through the speakers in the club. Me and Aruba started shaking our asses, and I was in my zone. That was the perfect thing about being young. You can live life the way that you want, and no fucks were given at all.

This cutie came up behind me, and I bent my ass over, twerking nice and slow on his dick. I could feel him get hard underneath my ass, and I was enjoying it.

"Aye, my mans, I need you to back up off my pussy," a deep voice rang out.

I stopped dancing and looked behind me. Trill was standing there glaring at dude, and I was confused. I had been watching him all night popping bottles in the VIP area and letting the strippers twerk on him.

"My bad, Trill, I ain't know that was you," the dude said and immediately backed away.

I chuckled as I stared at Tril. He wrapped his arms around my waist and pulled me close.

"Ion like that shit," he said in a husky tone.

"When did I become your pussy? I belong to no one," I shot back. "Once I fucked, that became mine, shawty. What's good with it,

though? You couldn't hit a nigga's line?" he asked, and I stared at his fine ass.

"A phone works both ways, shawty," I shot back, and he laughed

"You always got some smart mouth shit to say." He kissed me on my cheek. His lips were warm, and he made me feel all tingly inside.

"I'm just saying, my nigga. But, what's up?" I eyed him.

"You don't miss me yet? I haven't stopped thinking about that juicy shit since I hit," he stated, and I laughed.

"Boy, fuck you! You don't fuck with me. You ain't even hit my line.

So, whatever," I told him.

"Man, look. I be bussing moves left and right. Believe me, though, you run through my mind constantly."

"Nigga, you laying it on thick! It's only been two days." He laughed.

"Shawty, I'm real as fuck, and I'm telling you, for these last two days, I haven't stop thinking about yo' ass."

"Mhmmmm." I turned my lip up. "But, whatchu about to do?" he asked. "Me and my sister are going…"

I was stopped mid-sentence when I heard gunshots ring out

Pow, pow, pow

"Get down!" Trill shouted and pulled me down, but he couldn't keep me down. I had to find Ru.

She had walked off once I started dancing with Trill. I hopped up and ran toward where me and Ru was at, and in the midst of it she was running toward me. I hugged her tightly and we grabbed hands and ran toward the door, I didn't even look for Trill, my only concern was my sister and our safety. It was pandemonium, and I just wanted to make it out of the fucking club alive.

Once we were outside, we ran toward the parking lot. Me and Aruba hugged, and I headed for my car as she hopped in her car.

"Call me when you make it home," I yelled out to her as she pulled off. "Aye!"

I looked up, and Trill was running my way.

"You dropped your phone, shawty." He smirked and handed me my phone that I didn't know I dropped.

"Oh my God, thanks so much. I'm sorry for running off like that, but I had to find my sister."

"Nah, you good, shawty. I already know how that shit

is. You enjoy your night, and be careful out here," he said and walked off.

I got in my car and drove off, heading to my apartment. I couldn't get Trill's sexy smile off my mind.

Chapter: 5 Aspen

Tears raced down my face as I got dressed this morning. I couldn't even bring myself to get out of bed, but I knew if I stayed home, I would be depressed thinking about Finesse.

It had been a week since he'd been home, and it was fucking me. He'd never stayed with her for a fucking week! The disrespect was becoming too much now. I wiped my tears with the back of my hand and continued to get dressed.

After dressing, I left the crib. I sat in my car contemplating my next move. I had to open the massage parlor by 10:00 am, but I was early as always. Finally making a decision, I opened my phone and put Finesse's iCloud information in the Where's My iPhone? app. I knew his information because I helped him set it up when he first got his phone. His location popped up, and I started my ignition then peeled off, heading in the direction of the location. It didn't give me the exact location, but close by was good enough for me. Fuck that, he was gonna bring his ass home. I wasn't tolerating it any longer.

When I pulled up on 77th and Calumet, there was a bunch of houses. I didn't know which one to go to, so I did the next best thing. I honked my horn like a fucking mad woman. As I laid on the horn, people came out of their houses looking at me like I was fucking crazy. Shit, I was crazy because a man had made me this way. I hopped out my car and looked around.

"Finesse!!" I shouted at the top of my lungs "Finesse!" I

screamed again.

I looked around, and door of the house to the left of me came open. Finesse walked out with a wife beater on, some jeans, and some house shoes. My anger went up ten notches. He frowned as he walked up on me.

"Bitch, have you lost ya fucking mind?" he growled through gritted teeth.

"Nah, have you?"

"Aspen, take ya dumb ass to work! Fuck is you doing here?"

"The question is what are you doing here? I'm your woman, and you haven't been home in a week. You haven't answered my phone calls or nothing! What are we doing Finesse?" I said as my voice cracked.

I loved him so much it was sickening.

"I needed a break. I need you to leave, Aspen, and go open my business. That's money for me and you, and you out here acting a fucking fool."

"Come home, Finesse. This is not how we solve our problems," I told him.

God, why couldn't I shake this man? I hated how he made me feel, I hated what he was doing to me, and I hated that I was so fucking weak when it came to him.

"Really, Finesse? You gon' talk to this bitch right in front of my house," a light skinned chick with a big ass booty said, coming out the house in some athletic wear.

She had on leggings and a tank top. She was beautiful, and I almost felt insecure after seeing her. So, this was her.

"Kari, go back in the crib," he snapped on her, and I smirked

"Bitch, do I come to your house? Huh?" the girl shouted at

me, and I laughed.

"Bitch, go back in the house like he said. Grown folks are talking," I spat.

"Bitch, what?" She tried to run up on me, but Finesse stood in front of

her

"Take ya dumb ass back in the house, Kari, and I ain't gon' say the shit

again!" Finesse yelled.

"Yeah, bitch, take ya dumb ass back in the house before I fuck you up!" I threatened, and then she laughed.

"Girl, fuck you! After you're done spilling ya heart out, I'm gonna fuck our man into a coma while you go slave at his job." She smirked.

That sent me over the edge. I guess the truth hurt because I was hurt by what she just said to me. Finesse was protecting her, but that didn't mean shit to me. I reached over him and grabbed her ass by that curly ass weave. I dragged her to the ground, and I proceeded to beat the shit out of her ass.

"Aspen! Aspen! Chill the fuck out! Yo, chill the fuck out," Finesse yelled, trying to pull me off her, but I was a raging bull, and my grip was a death grip.

I was trying to rip that bitch's hair from her scalp. As I proceeded to lay hands on her, the next thing I knew, I felt a stinging sensation across my face.

Whap!

Finesse smacked the shit out of me, and it broke me from my trance. I looked up at him, and he was fuming.

"I said let her the fuck go!" he growled.

I stood up and backed away. Ole girl was lying on the ground bleeding from the mouth. Her light skin was flushed red, and she was crying.

"You hit me because of this bitch!" I shouted at him.

"Nah, I hit you because you wasn't listening! Damn, take ya ass to work, Aspen! And you take yo' no fighting ass in the fucking house, Kari! Y'all bitches get on my fucking nerves! Damn!" he shouted and walked off.

I stared at him, and tears welled up in my eyes. This was too fucking much for me right now. I walked off and got back in my car. After I started my ignition, I peeled away as tears fell from my eyes.

SITTING behind the front desk at the massage parlor, I wasn't in the mood. My attitude was fucked up now. After the fight this morning with Finesse's bitch, I couldn't pull myself outta my funk.

"Girl, that police muthafucka got the whole damn room smelling like corn chips. I can't stand his stanky foot ass!" Asia scoffed, coming into the front.

I looked at her and rolled my eyes. "Get used to it. It's ya job," I snapped.

"What's wrong with you, bitch?" She instantly copped an attitude.

I didn't intend to come off mean, but I wasn't in the mood to be hearing that complaining shit. I didn't tell my sisters what transpired this morning because all they would say was that I was stupid, and I didn't feel like hearing it.

"Ain't shit wrong. I'm good."

"Obviously not, but you know what? I ain't gon' even stress you about your business, bitch. Fuck you and your attitude," she snapped and walked off.

We went through the rest of the day not really saying shit to each other. By closing time, I sat at the desk counting the money made for the week, and we had made our 350,000 quota.

"I'm about to get ready and leave." Aruba came to the office door and said.

"Oh, okay," I said and handed over her cut of the money. She flipped through her stack of money and smiled. "Thanks, sis."

"Give this to Asia," I said and handed her Asia's money, but she didn't grab it.

"Uh uh, bitch, don't put me in that petty shit. Give sis her money. She ain't do nothing to you," she stated, and I rolled my eyes.

"Girl, whatever." I grabbed Asia's money and put the rest of the money in the safe.

After I locked up the office, me and Ru headed back to the front of the building. Asia was letting the last girl out, and then she locked the door.

I walked over and gave her money to her.

"Thanks, you moody bitch," she said, and we all laughed.

That's what I loved about my sisters. We were able to get past certain shit.

There was a knock on the front door that got all of our attention. It was Dyna, one of the girls who worked there. She must have left something. I unlocked the door for her, and she was pushed inside by three niggas with ski masks on.

"Where the money at, bitch?" one of the gunmen growled, aiming his banger in my face.

"Oh my God," Aruba shouted and ran over to me.

Asia was stuck in place, and tears fell from her eyes. Dyna

was crying and shaking so badly. My heart rate increased, and I felt my blood pressure go up a thousand notches. I was scared shitless

"I... I don't have any money." My voice trembled as we all huddled together in the corner.

There were three of them, and the biggest one looked intimidating as hell. I couldn't see his face, but his eyes were dark. They didn't seem to have any light in them.

"Bitch, where the fuck is the money?" He growled and grabbed me by my hair then pressed his gun to my head.

"Oh God, please! Please don't hurt her!" Asia cried, and tears streamed down my face.

He was gonna kill me.

"Shut the fuck up!" another gun man yelled at Asia.

He walked over like he was about to hit her or something, but the third nigga, who was off in the cut stopped him. He didn't talk; he just grabbed him and pulled him back.

"It's in the safe! Just take it! It's all in the safe," Aruba blurted out.

Fuck! I knew Finesse was gonna be pissed the fuck off after this. I just hoped like hell that I lived long enough to tell the story.

"Go open the safe. Take that bitch to the back to open it," he instructed one of the men, referring to Ru.

"She can't open it. I'm the only one with the code," I mentioned. "Let's fucking go," the dude holding the gun said.

I got off my knees, and we headed to the office. Once in the office, I trembled as I fucked with the numbers. I kept getting them wrong, even when I knew the code.

"Bitch, if you play games with me, that nigga gonna be picking ya brains up off this floor," he threatened.

Finally, I got the code right. I knew this nigga wasn't playing. He didn't show an ounce of remorse. Once the safe was opened, I placed the money in a black garbage bag.

"Why, why are you doing this?" I had to ask him.

Finesse had so much more money in different places. Why did they pick this one?

"Shut the fuck up!" he growled before he grabbed the money and led me back into the front where everybody else was located.

I looked over at my sisters and Dyna. They were crying their eyes out.

We all were scared. We all believed that we were gonna die.

"You have the money. Can y'all please leave? I swear we won't call the police, I swear," Aruba begged them.

The other two stick up dudes ran out the door, but the dude holding the gun on me still hadn't moved.

"You Finesse's bitch?" he asked me, and I slowly nodded. "You coming with me," he demanded.

"What? No! No! No!" I shouted as he led me out of the front and into a waiting van.

I tried to fight him off, but he didn't budge. His strength was serious.

This nigga was about to kill me all because of Finesse.

When we got to the van, I tried to plead with him, but he wasn't trying to hear it.

"Didn't I say shut up, bitch?" he growled and clocked me in the head with the butt of his gun, causing me to black out in an instant.

Chapter: 6 Gangsta

After getting shawty situated at the motel room, I stood in the parking lot smoking my blunt. Trill was staring at me, and Menace was caking on the phone in the corner with Fallon. I had

a connect who got me rooms at the Motel 6. All I had to do was slide them a couple of dollars, and they were down for whatever I had going on. I was able to get through the emergency exit so that other guests wouldn't see. Shit always worked out in my favor.

"Nigga, what the fuck was that!" Trill snapped at me.

I didn't say anything as I let my thoughts take control of my mind. I knew what the fuck I was doing. That nigga Finesse was gonna pay the fuck up. If he wanted his bitch back, he was gonna come off that muthafucking bread.

"Nigga, that nigga Finesse gonna pay for the hoe. Don't worry." I shrugged.

"That wasn't part of the plan. When did we fucking start kidnapping bitches? Trill was visibly upset, but he would get over it.

"Nigga, don't question my fucking motives! I do what the fuck I wanna do!"

"Nah, muthafucka, I thought we were a team. You got some pussy ass vendetta against that bitch ass nigga Finesse, and you dragged us into the shit. I don't get down like that, and you fucking know it," Trill yelled.

I just looked at him. He was right, but I didn't give a fuck.

"Man, shut the fuck up. Acting like a bitch," I snarled, and he walked up on me.

These niggas stayed wanting to fight.

"What the fuck you just say, nigga?" he snarled through gritted teeth.

I looked down at him and smirked. If he knew like I knew, he would get the fuck outta my face and go about his business.

"Trill, you my homie, but if you swing on me, nigga, you ain't gon' be nobody's homie 'cause I'm gon dead yo ass if you don't get the fuck outta my face, my nigga," I told him in a calm voice.

He knew I meant every word. I didn't play games out here in these streets.

"Aye, bro, y'all niggas cool the fuck out. Shit, we got the bag. That's the only thing that fucking matters. Fuck them hoes," Menace said.

I looked at him and didn't say shit.

"Y'all niggas didn't even know that ole girl you tried to smack up, Menace, that's my shawty. And the one you kidnapped is her fucking sister!"

"Wait, what, nigga? You ain't tell me you knew them bitches!" I shouted.

That's why he was so fucking quiet during the heist. The nigga ain't mumble a fucking word the entire time we were there. He couldn't risk shawty hearing his voice.

"Damn, my nigga, what the fuck?" Menace said in a low tone.

"Yeah, nigga! I hope she didn't recognize my eyes or no

crazy shit that women be on," he scoffed.

"Nigga, you were supposed to say something. Damn."

Now, I felt bad, and I rarely felt bad about anything I did. I figured, fuck 'em.

"Nigga, I didn't know she worked there. I really don't know that much about shawty, but she got some good pussy." He smirked, and we all laughed.

"Nah, for real, though, nigga. Whatchu gon' do about shawty? That nigga Finesse ain't gon' take it too well that you got his bitch." Trill chuckled.

"Fuck him. If he wants her back, he gon' pay. Simple as that."

I finished chatting it up with them niggas, and then they left. Bracing myself, I headed in the motel room. I didn't have on my ski mask or nothing like that because, frankly, I don't give a fuck if shawty saw my face. Finesse was a bitch, and I was about to pull his hoe card.

When I entered the room, shawty was tied to the bed post, I had her mouth taped. She was wide awake with tears running down her face. When she saw me, her eyes widened. She was scared shitless. I wasn't gonna hurt her, though. I didn't have a need to. I just needed her as leverage.

I sat on the edge of the bed and looked at her. "I'm gon' take the tape off your mouth. If you scream, I'm gonna fuck you up. Understand?" I told her in a threatening tone, and she nodded.

I pulled the tape off her mouth, and she just looked at me.

Damn, she was beautiful. She had some big, bold, light hazel eyes. Her chocolate skin complexion was rich and smooth like a Hershey's, she was thick as fuck in all the right places, and the ponytail she sported brought out an innocence in her face.

"Please.... can you just let me go?" she said, and her voice trembled.

I was thinking about letting her go if she cooperated with a nigga, but if she didn't, Finesse was gonna have to bury her. I didn't say anything as I got up from the bed and walked over to my bookbag then pulled out the burner cell that I had just brought earlier. Walking back over to the bed, I plopped down and looked at her with a serious expression etched on my face.

"What's ya nigga's number?" I asked, and she gave me his digits.

I pressed call and went into the bathroom. The nigga didn't answer the first time I called, so I dialed him back. He instantly picked up.

"Who the fuck is this?" he growled.

I could tell he probably got the news about his shit being robbed and his bitch being snatched up. I put a t-shirt over the phone to muffle my voice.

"Nigga, I got yo bitch," I snarled and opened the bathroom door. I walked into the room and put his shawty on the phone.

"Fi… Finesse… Finesse, Baby—"

"Bae! Bae! Hol' on, I'm coming for you," he yelled.

"I'm scared, baby…" she cried, and I snatched the phone from her goofy ass.

She had nothing to be crying about, but I guess I was an intimidating looking ass nigga.

"Pussy ass nigga—" He tried to say, but I cut his bitch ass off.

"I want five million. If you don't have my bread in three days, I'm killing this bitch," I snarled and hung up the phone.

She looked at me and started violently shaking.

"Please… I have nothing to do with whatever you and

Finesse have going on. I have my parents and my sisters who are going to be looking for me. I'm sorry about whatever is going on, but please don't hurt me," she cried, and I ignored her.

"I'll advise you to shut the fuck up before I tape ya mouth back," I spat, and she shut the fuck up as she quietly let the tears roll down her face.

I took off my shirt and sat in the chair. Then I grabbed the remote and turned the television on. An old ass Jamie Foxx Show rerun was on. I kicked off my boots and got comfortable in the chair. We were gonna be there for a while, that I knew for sure. I also knew that Finesse cheap ass wasn't about to pay for his bitch back. I just wanted to fuck with his mind a little. The money would've been good, but I was fucking rich already. I didn't need his shit.

I hated that nigga Finesse, and I was gonna show him just how much I hated his ass. I was about to hit his pockets when he least expected it. Shawty was still crying, and I felt bad that I was gonna end her muthafucking life when this shit was all over.

"Aye, you hungry?" I asked, and she bawled even harder.

"Fuck it then. I was gonna order a pizza or some shit, but if you ain't hungry, I can't force ya dumb ass to eat."

I shrugged then ordered my pizza and a two-liter Pepsi. As I got comfortable in the chair, I thought about all the ways I could make Finesse's life a lil bit harder.

I LEANED against my car smoking my blunt with my mind in deep thought. I had been living my life so fast that I didn't know when I was gonna sit the fuck down. Always on the go, always straight to the money. Shit was getting real out here, and honestly, I was getting tired. I lost a little bit of myself every day out in these streets.

Currently, I was waiting for the first half of my payment. Kozlov had set up the meeting with one of his runners.

The parking lot of the motel was dark, and I inhaled the blunt as I waited. I spotted a black BMW pull up. The car doors opened, and two figures stepped out the car. My gun was on my waist, and I waited with anticipation to see who it was. Never the type to be too trusting, I always stayed on point. From the walk, I could tell it was a woman coming my way. The heels of her stilettos clacked against the pavement as she inched closer to me.

"Geon," Lanay spoke with a smile etched on her face, and I drew my gun from my waistband.

"Bitch, the fuck you doing here?" I growled as I eyed her up and down with the gun aimed at her face.

A look of fear crept across her face. She didn't know what to think. I never thought I would see her in a million years, and I didn't think she would have the audacity to show her face to me. I hated this bitch.

"I came to deliver the money to you... that's it." She heled her hands up, but that didn't mean shit to me.

I bit my bottom lip hard as fuck, but before I could pull the trigger, my phone rang. I pulled it out, and it was Kozlov.

"What?" I barked.

This motherfucker set me up. He knew who he was sending to bring me the money.

"Not now, Young Gangsta. You will get your chance for vengeance.

Business first, and personal later," he spoke then hung up the phone.

He knew I wanted to murder her. If no one else knew how I felt about Lanay, Kozlov who did. I talked to him a lot when I was locked up.

Snatching the manila envelope out of her hands, I checked to see if all my money was there. I knew that it was because Kozlov knew not to play with my money.

"I'm… I'm sorry, Geon, for what I did to you. I know it might not mean much to you, but I'm so fucking sorry. I had to do it. I had to save myself and our son," she said, and my eyes widened

"What?"

She had tears falling from her eyes and she shook her head in an up and down motion.

"You lying bitch! Get the fuck outta my face before I blow yo' brains all over this fucking parking lot! Lying ass bitch!" I spat, and she jumped.

"I'm not lying, but if you wanna see your son, just ask Kozlov for my number, and he will give it to you," she said and stormed off.

I stood there stuck in place in the parking lot wondering what the fuck just happened. After not seeing her after all these years, I thought that I would hate her so much, but I didn't, and I that shit felt weird to me.

My cell buzzed, and it was a text message from Kozlov.

Get the Job done!

After reading the text message, I went back into the motel room, and the chick, Aspen, was up. She was still sad and shit. I felt bad, but then again, I didn't. I took my gun out and aimed in her direction.

"Oh My God! Oh My God!" she cried and closed her eyes tight as fuck.

She put her head down and started praying. That shit fucked with my head. I couldn't do it, not right now at least. She was so beautiful, and I knew deep down inside that she was innocent in whatever this was. I was a pawn, and so was she.

"Lift ya head up. You get to live another night," I told her and walked out the motel room.

I knew eventually I had to get the job done since I had already been paid half the money to do it. And I didn't need any issues with Kozlov. Shawty could at least get a little time to make peace.

Chapter: 7 Trill

My mind was fucked up as I sat in my apartment thinking about Asia. She was scared as fuck when me and my niggas ran up in that spot. I had no idea she worked there

nor her sisters. I didn't intentionally do that shit. If I had known that it was her peoples spot, I would've told Gangsta that it wasn't a good heist to go on.

I divided up the money, and we didn't come off with shit but 350 G's. That was chump change, and I knew for a fact that Gangsta had some other shit up his sleeve. I hated to be left in the dark. That's not how I operated. I wanted a muthafucka to keep it all the way real with me.

He was my nigga till the world blow, but I wouldn't hesitate to cut him the fuck off. I looked at my cell, and I wanted to call Asia so bad, but I just didn't have the words to say to her. I knew that Gangsta still had shawty with him, and that shit was crazy. It was like ever since he came back from DC, he was a different person. Something happened to him out there, and he was now bitter as fuck.

Instead of calling Asia, I turned on the news. I laid across my couch and tried to relax my mind. My cell started vibrating, and it was my moms. I looked at it, but I didn't answer. She liked to call and start preaching to me about shit, and I wasn't in the mood to hear it. She called back to back, yet I didn't answer. This was nothing new for her. She did this shit all the time.

As I continued to watch the news a Breaking News headline came across the screen.

"This is Howard Hughes reporting live from Channel 7 news. There are reports from Loyola University in Chicago's Rogers Park neighborhood that there is an active shooter on the campus," the reporter said.

I sat up, and as soon as I did, my mother started calling my phone back. I answered then.

"Yeah, Ma?" My heart rate increased. That was the school my brother and Asia attended. '

"Rahmeek! Rico has been shot," she cried, and I could hear the worry in her voice.

"What? I'm on my way! Where he at?" I asked her as my nerves got the best of me. I was fumbling around trying to put on my shit and look for my car keys.

"We're at Northwestern Hospital downtown. They have him in surgery." She was crying, and my heart broke to listen to my mother's voice. I didn't need this shit right now.

Once I had my shit on, I was out the door. I hopped in my car and sped as fast as I could to the hospital. Going through the emergency department, I spotted my moms and some more parents.

"What happened, Ma?" I asked her.

"Son, I don't know. I don't know. All I heard was a student opened fire on campus. He's shot seven students so far, and Rico was one of them. I'm so scared, Rahmeek. I can't lose my baby boy," she cried.

I hugged my moms tight. It was only 11:00 in the morning, and my day was starting off fucked up already. This shit couldn't be happening right now.

All I could think about was if it was my fault why this happened to my lil brother. Was this my karma for all the bad shit I did in my fucking life?

After waiting about three hours, the doctor finally came out to talk to me and my moms.

"Your son, Rahmeek, is doing just fine. The bullet didn't hit any major organs, but he was bleeding internally, and the process to stop the bleeding was a long one. But, he's stable, and he's gonna be fine," the doctor said, and my mother broke down in tears. I had to pick her up off the floor.

"Thanks, Doc, I appreciate that. We appreciate that." I shook his hand. "Can we go see him now?"

"Give him about an hour, and then you can go on back. He's fresh out of the operating room. So, his anesthesia will have to wear off, and he has to come to," he told us, and I nodded.

Thank God. I would've probably gone crazy if my lil brother didn't make it out of this one. I had seen so many doctors coming to tell some of the families from the shooting that their loved ones didn't make it, and that shit broke my heart.

As we waited, I scan my phone and texted Nika back. She was concerned because she saw the news segment as well. I heard a voice that made me look up. It was Asia, and she was at the nurse's station asking about Rico.

"Asia," I called out.

She spotted me then came over and threw her arms my around my neck.

"Oh my god, is he okay?" She had a tear stained face, and I only nodded.

"Yeah, he's good. He just came out of surgery."

"Oh, thank God! I'm so sorry that happened. I don't know what the hell was going on. All I know is I was in class, and then they put the school on lockdown because someone was shooting. When they finally let us out of the class, I found out that Rico had been shot." She mouthed the words so fast and she was shaking so badly that I hugged her tight to get her to calm down.

"He's cool, A, he's cool," I whispered as she sobbed in my chest. "Come, on you need some fresh air." I grabbed her hand and walked

her outside. "You aight?"

"No! Everything is going wrong right now! My sister was kidnapped by some fucking maniac who robbed her massage parlor. We haven't heard from her, and we're on pins and needles. Her weak ass boyfriend told us not to go to the police because he's gonna handle it and to go on about my fucking life, but I can't! And then Rico gets shot! This shit is horrible right now, and I'm stressing the fuck out right now. I'm too young for this shit!" she cried.

She was fucking beautiful. Yeah, in the beginning, I only wanted to fuck, but seeing her vulnerable like this made me see her differently.

I took my thumbs and wiped away her tears. I kissed the top of her forehead then grabbed her and hugged her tightly.

"It's gonna be okay, Lips. I bet she's good. If the police ain't came and said they found a body, then think positive. Hopefully, her nigga is a man of his word, and he do what the fuck he said he gonna do to get her back. Think positive, ma, that's all you can do." I tried to comfort her, but I knew that shit was fucking with her.

"I'm trying, Trill, I swear I am."

We walked to my car, and I rolled a blunt. We both needed to get high to take our minds off the bullshit.

"Besides the bullshit, how's life been treating you? I haven't heard from you since I saw you the club that day."

"Life is life, and I'm gonna tell you the same thing I told you when we were at the club. A phone works both ways. You can pick that muthafucka up to call and text just like I can."

"You right, ma, and I'm gon' do better because I'm tryna get to know you better."

"You sure it ain't all about the pussy?" she joked, and I laughed.

"Nah it's about the pussy, but it's also about that smile, that personality, and much more," I told her honestly, and she smiled.

"Well, I'll be waiting for yo call, but let me get back in the hospital. I wanna talk to one of the girls who I had class with sister to see how she's doing," she said and handed me the blunt back.

"Aight, ma. I'll be back in there in a minute, so we can go see lil bro," I told her, and she nodded.

Asia got out the car, and I exhaled deeply. It was fucked up knowing that I knew who had her sister. I knew for a fact that Gangsta wasn't gonna hurt her, but it was time for the nigga to let the bitch go. This shit was getting out of hand.

I picked up my cell and dialed Gangsta's number. He answered on the first ring.

"What's good, broski? I just saw the news. Is Rico good?" he asked in a hurried tone.

"Nah, man, he got shot. We at the hospital right now, me and my moms."

"Aww, fuck, man. What they saying?"

"He just came out of surgery, and he's stable, so that's a good thing. We're just waiting to visit him, but what's up with you, nigga?" I inquired.

"Whatchu mean?"

"I mean, what's up? You still got shawty?" I asked.

"Hell yeah, and the bitch is a pain in my ass with all this fucking crying she doing."

"What her nigga saying?"

"He ain't saying much. I know that nigga, though. He ain't tryna come off no fucking bread for shawty."

"So whatchu gon' do?" I asked. "Lights out, nigga."

"Nah, man, her sister was just hitting me up crying and shit about her.

Don't do that shit, nigga. Let her go," I pleaded with him.

"I can't do that, nigga. She saw my face, and I ain't going to jail over no bitch. I don't give a fuck how fine she is," he said, and I smirked.

Where that shit come from?

"Nigga, fine? I doubt the bitch want yo ass after you done kidnapped her. Bro, yo' ass is fucking crazy." I chuckled as I listened to him.

"Man, I ain't saying I want the bitch, I'm just saying she fine as fuck though," he said and laughed.

"Yo ass sick in the head. Where you at, nigga?"

"Heading to Ihop to get her ass some breakfast," He said and I really burst into laughter.

"Oh, you taking care of her." "I mean, shorty gotta eat, bro."

"Man, look, let her go. You know that nigga Finesse ain't about to pay that ransom, and her people are worried sick about her ass."

"I'm gon' let her go, but first I need to see what the nigga gon' do. He might just come through for her ass if he really loves her," he said.

I doubted it. That nigga was lame as fuck, and he fucked with all types of bitches in the hood. He couldn't care less about his shawty, and that's some real shit.

"Aight, bro, I'm about to go see about Rico. I'll hit yo' ass up later to see what's what," I told him and hung up the phone.

I got out of my car and headed back into the hospital. I needed Gangsta to get his shit in order. We didn't need a kidnapping nor a murder on us right now. We were living the good life, and he was fucking that shit up by being weak as fuck. He was bitter, and I wanted to know the fuck why.

My main concern right now, though, was my lil brother. I needed to make sure he was good, and the first thing he was gonna do when he got better was transfer fucking schools. Fuck that. If he would've died, there wouldn't have been no more fucking Loyola because I was gonna burn that bitch to the ground.

Chapter: 8 Asia

Shit has been on my mind heavy lately. My good friend, Rico, was shot, and that was fucking with me. Rico was a good dude, him and Trill. Speaking of Trill, I couldn't get his sexy ass off

my mind neither. I wanted to see him again. He was so affectionate toward me the day I came to the hospital, and I liked the softer side of him. But that lovey dovey shit would have to wait. I was focused on getting Aspen back.

I never thought that I would be a part of a school shooting and a robbery in the same week. Since that whole robbery shit went down, shit has been intense. Finesse still hadn't come up with any more information, and I was irritated by it all.

"Why the fuck this nigga ain't answering his phone!" I growled as I pressed end on my cell.

I was pacing the in Aruba's living room as I attempted to call Finesse, but he'd been ignoring my phone calls.

"I don't know, but I say we ride down on his ass," Ru suggested, and she was right.

"He got us fucked up! Our fucking sister is missing, and he ain't answering his phone or telling us shit! He asked us not to go to the police, and we haven't, thinking his bitch ass was gonna do something about her being missing, but he's still coming up empty handed! Nah, fuck that! Something has to give!" I stressed.

"Yeah, he's blowing me. He knows something and he's not telling. It's been fucking five days!" Ru yelled.

"Come on, bitch. Grab yo shit and the baseball bats. He's gonna give us answers or we're gonna fuck him up. It's just that simple," I told her.

She looked at me like I was crazy, but I was dead ass serious.

Something had to give. Nobody was gonna keep giving me sob ass story when it came to my sister. Talking about he's doing the best he can.

He had the massage parlor back open, and he expected us to come back to work. We didn't, so he had Dyna running the joint. That bitch made me believe she had something to do with it. She was back on the job like nothing ever happened.

Aruba got dressed, and once she was dressed, we were out the door. We got in my car, and I peeled off toward Aspen and Finesse's house. It took us about twenty minutes to make it out to the suburbs where they lived.

Getting out of the car, I spotted Finesse's truck. "He's home," I said to Ru, and she nodded.

I rang the doorbell, and it took him a minute to answer. Finesse came to the door, and I barged in his house without an invitation. He had us fucked up. This was my sister's house as well.

Closing the door, he turned to look at us. "What the fuck y'all want?" he snarled.

"We wanna know what the fuck are you doing to find my sister!" I yelled.

"I'm doing everything I can. The fuck you mean?" he snapped back, but I wasn't hearing that lame shit.

"Well, it's not enough! What if something happened to her? You opened the massage parlor back up and went on with life like you don't give a fuck! It's been five days, Finesse! Fucking Five!" Aruba screamed at him.

"Y'all bitches ain't in the streets. Y'all don't know how this shit goes! I got my ear to the streets every muthafucking day, and I keep coming up empty handed!" he replied.

"Bitches? Finesse, don't make me fuck you up! I'm not Aspen! Don't disrespect me!" I snapped at his bitch ass.

I didn't know who the fuck he thought he was talking too, but I wasn't the one.

"Baby, what's all the commotion going on down here?" a light skinned chick said as she came down the stairs.

My mouth dropped open. I couldn't believe he had the audacity to bring a bitch in my sister's home. He hung his head and didn't say shit.

"Bitch, if you know like I know, you would leave right now! You're in my sister's fucking house, and I'm ten seconds away from smashing yo ass," I threatened.

She looked at me and smiled.

"This is my man's house, and this is my man," she shot back.

I ran up on her and dragged her down the stairs. Finesse picked me up and took me outside before I could get a good grip on the bitch. I could hear Aruba arguing with ole girl. Once outside, I looked at Finesse and frowned.

"You a disrespectful ass nigga! My sister could be fucking dead somewhere, and you got a ratchet ass bitch in her house! Nigga, I oughta have some niggas come fuck you up!" I glared at him.

"Man, look, me and Aspen been having problems, but I love my girl. And yeah, ole girl is here, but she ain't slept in this house! You think I'll disrespect my girl like that? She came over to check on me! That's it, man! She knows I love my woman, and

I'm doing everything I can to find Aspen. That's on my father's grave," he said, and I didn't believe him.

Tears came to my eyes as I thought about how I hadn't seen my sister nor heard her voice in a week. I thought about the many times she'd cried when he'd hurt her, and now it's a bitch in her house!

"Ru!" I hollered.

She came flying out the front door and looked between me and Finesse.

"What's up?"

"Pop the trunk," I told her, and she nodded.

Finesse looked confused as I glared at him. Ru went to the car, popped the trunk, and came back with the baseball bats.

She handed me one, and she had the other.

"You got two minutes to tell that bitch to leave, or I'm about to fuck up everything in this driveway," I threatened.

He looked at me and laughed.

"Get the fuck off my property, man. When I hear something concerning, Aspen. I'll be sure to let y'all know. But if y'all ain't got shit else to do, get the fuck on," he snapped.

I cocked my head to the side. He walked off and went back in the house, slamming his front door in the process, as if to say fuck us. He called my bluff. And that was something he shouldn't have done.

I looked at Aruba then took the baseball bat and went over to his cocaine white Range Rover. I swung the bat as hard as I could, smashing the back window. Ru took her bat and smashed the side window, and the alarm started blaring. The front door opened, and Finesse came back on the porch with a gun in his hands.

"Get the fuck off my property before I shoot one of you

bitches right fucking now!" he growled.

I heard him, I saw the gun, and I still didn't give a fuck. If this was gonna catch his attention, then so be it.

"Fuck you, bitch ass nigga! Find my muthafucking sister! It's your fault she's in this shit! Find her, or I'm going to the police, bitch!" I screamed as I walked to the front of the Range Rover.

I took the bat and smashed the front window. Finesse let off a gun shot in the air. Ru grabbed my wrist and started running.

She was scared, but I wasn't. That bitch ass nigga was gonna find my sister, or I was gonna make his life a living fucking hell. As me and Aruba drove away, I burst into tears. Ru rubbed my hand as she drove, and I couldn't stop crying.

"Don't cry, A, she's gonna be good. I feel it. She's okay," she tried to assure me.

"If she's hurt, I don't know what I'll do. This is so fucked up, man, so fucked up!" I sobbed.

"It is, but Aspen is a fighter. She got this, sis. I know she does."

"If Finesse don't find our sister, I'm gonna kill him. I promise you, Ru, I'm gonna kill him," I said in a low tone as I wiped my tears with the back of my hand.

It was all his fault. When the kidnappers asked her was she Finesse bitch, I knew then that all this shit went down because of him

Chapter: 9 Aspen

I was shivering my ass off in this hotel room. This nigga had the damn central air on like he was crazy. It was the middle of September, and the weather was cooling off. This was

Chicago. The weather was funny as fuck. I knew I was bound to get a cold or something fucking with him.

His ass was sleeping in the fucking chair. I had counted the days, and I had been sitting in this hotel room for five days straight. I hadn't washed my ass or changed my clothes. I felt dirty as hell, and this nigga was irritating.

"Hey!" I called out to him.

He instantly opened his eyes. I guessed he was a light sleeper. "Whaddup?" He yawned as he stood and stretched.

"I have to use the bathroom," I told him.

I needed to find a way to get the fuck up out of there, but he was a big nigga, and I couldn't take the chance of running, and he did something to me.

"Aight."

He walked over and untied me from the bedpost. Once I was loose, I went in the bathroom and closed the door. I stood in front of the bathroom mirror and looked at my appearance. My pony tail was all over my head. My eyes had bags underneath them, and they were swollen from all the crying I had been doing. I shook my head as I looked myself over.

"This can't be life right now," I whispered.

I was trapped in a sleazy ass hotel with a psychotic muthafucka who had a vendetta against Finesse. And speaking of Finesse, this nigga hadn't even bothered to pay the ransom. What was supposed to be three days had now turned into five. I didn't know if I was gonna live or die, and at this point, I didn't care.

"Aye!" the nigga banged on the door, causing me to jump.

I hadn't even used the bathroom yet. I cracked the door, and looking at him, I didn't know what to think.

His caramel skin complexion was flushed red as if he was angry or something. He had tattoos on his face, which gave him a scary feel, and it was a long scar underneath his eye. It reminded me of Scar from The Lion King. This nigga stood 6'5" and he was buff as hell. He was big and intimidating looking. But he was so damn fine, and that right there bothered me the most. I shouldn't be attracted to him.

Although he had me trapped in this hotel room, he wasn't mean to me. He was calm and quiet. He fed me, and he asked me constantly if I was good. He seemed to have so much concern for me, and as crazy as it may sound, I appreciated it.

He put me in the mind of the rapper The Game. I mean, he looked identical to him, as if he was his lost brother. And it was cray that his name was Gangsta. His swag screamed gangsta. He had an aura that screamed he wasn't supposed to be fucked with, but that turned me on. And I shouldn't be turned on. This shit was crazy. Hell, I think I was going crazy.

"Yes?" I eyed him.

"What's good? It don't take that long to piss. Fuck you trying to do?" he growled, and I frowned.

"What do you mean? I'm a woman. I take my time in the bathroom," I snapped back.

This was my first time snapping back at him, and I was scared to see what he was gonna say.

"Hurry the fuck up!" he barked.

I just stared at him. Nah, fuck that, I wasn't about to go another night without getting my ass in the shower.

"I'm about to take a shower," I said. "What?"

"You heard me, I'm about to take a shower because I refuse to go another night or day without washing my ass. I don't know what type of women you're used to dealing with, but this is not it. If you gonna kill me then just do it, but I'm getting in the shower," I argued, and he just stared at me.

"Man, just hurry the fuck up!" his voice boomed, and I shut the bathroom door.

A smirk spread across my face. I got what I wanted. I started the shower and hopped inside. This water hitting my skin was the best feeling ever. It felt like it had been years since I washed my ass. I took the towel that hung on the rack and the small bar of soap that the hotel provided, and I lathered up the towel. Tears fell from my eyes because I was miserable at this point.

After showering and pulling myself together, I didn't wanna put back on the same dirty ass clothes, so I wrapped the towel around me and exited the bathroom. I went back in the room, and he looked at me and then turned his head.

"Shorty, why the fuck you ain't got no fucking clothes on?" he growled.

"I'm not putting those clothes back on," I spat. I was sick of his shit.

"Yo, you got a smart-ass mouth for a muthafucka that's being kidnapped." He chuckled, and I smiled.

"I'm just saying, if you not gonna kill me, then show me some type of respect. Those clothes are dirty as fuck, and I refuse to put them back on."

"Aight, whatever's clever, ma, but I'm tying you back to this bed," he stated matter of factly.

"Fine." I plopped down on the bed and lay back.

The minute I lay back, the towel came open. My titties and pussy were on full display. Thank God my body was everything because I would have been totally embarrassed by him looking at me.

He hesitated as he came around and was about to tie me up. I guess it caught him off guard to see me naked.

"Nah, you straight. I ain't got to tie you back up. You ain't gon' run out the door, because if you do, I'm gon blow yo' shit loose," he threatened.

That right there let me know this muthafucka was not sane at all. I slowly nodded and wrapped myself back up with the towel.

He walked back to the chair that he was sitting in and turned on the television. The room was quiet as we watched a Tyler Perry movie. I was scared to move, scared to say anything after he just shut my ass down. But, I was curious to know more about him.

"Can I ask you a question?"

"No. Shut the fuck up and watch TV," he snapped, and I stared at him. He was truly an asshole. I ignored what he said and spoke again.

"Why are you doing this? What do I have to do with anything concerning you and Finesse?" I questioned.

"Didn't I just tell you to shut up?" he barked, but I wasn't moved by his loud, aggressive tone.

Fuck it, if I was gonna die, then I wished he would do the shit already. "You did, but I don't give a fuck! Let me the fuck go or kill me. Either way, who fucking cares? I'm sick of being here! I wanna go home! You fucking bastard, I wanna go home!" I cried as tears fell from my eyes.

He stared at me and shook his head before he got out of the chair and grabbed the gun off the dresser. My heart sank to my stomach; he was about to kill me. He grabbed the burner phone as well and handed it to me.

"Call ya nigga," he demanded, and I did what he said.

I dialed Finesse's number, and he picked up on the first ring. "What's good, pussy?" Finesse's voice boomed.

"Baby…" I sobbed upon hearing his voice.

"Bae! Bae!" he shouted. His voice was laced with concern.

"Please… please give them whatever they're asking for. He's gonna kill me, Finesse."

The dude Gangsta took the shirt that was on the chair and snatched the phone from me. He covered the phone with the shirt, I guess to disguise his voice.

"Pussy, have my money by three o'clock today, or she dies," Gangsta said, and Finesse was still on speaker.

"I ain't giving you shit, nigga. You had her this long, you ain't tryna kill her. Give me my bitch back, and I won't put a bullet in your head," Finesse spat, and Gangsta laughed.

"Three o'clock, or she's dead."

"Kill her then, nigga. Bitch probably set me up," Finesse spat and hung up the phone.

I stood up on wobbly legs and tried to walk to the bathroom, but I couldn't because I broke down right there at the door. I couldn't believe what he just said out of his mouth. He just didn't give a fuck about me.

"Oh My God," I sobbed loudly.

I was naked with nothing but a towel wrapped around

me, on the floor of a dirty ass motel, crying my heart out. The man I loved who, I thought would do anything for me, didn't give one shit if I lived or died.

"Pleaseeee, God help me!" I bawled my eyes out, and it felt good.

The hate I felt at that moment for Gangsta and Finesse was crazy. If I had a gun, I would kill them both for playing with my life. They didn't love me, but I had family who did love me.

"Aye, shorty, stop all that fucking crying. G up around this bitch," Gangsta spoke with a frown etched on his face.

I looked at him through blurry vision and chuckled. "Fuck you!"

I wiped my tears and sat there on the rug like a five-year-old child. I was lost at this point, and I just didn't care anymore. Gangsta aggressively picked me up from the floor, and I got scared.

I didn't know what he was gonna do to me when he tossed me on the bed and looked down at me with a grimace.

"Stop all that fucking crying, bruh. You see the nigga don't give a fuck about ya ass, so what the fuck you crying for? That shit ain't gon' change shit," he snapped.

The crazy shit about it was, he was right. My tears weren't gonna change anything. I sniffled and wiped my tears with the back of my hand.

"You're right," I said just above a whisper. He looked at me and smirked.

"Shit, I know I am. That nigga is a fuck boy, always has been." He shrugged and plopped down on the chair.

"So, since he's not gonna give you the money, whatchu gonna do to me?" I asked.

"I ain't gon' do shit to you, ma. You good, so stop worrying." He smirked.

Something about the way he said it sent chills down my spine, and I didn't believe him. Something told me that I wasn't gonna make it out of this hotel room alive. I felt it in my soul. I sat back on the bed and didn't shed another tear. I prayed. I prayed that God got me out of this mess. I didn't deserve this.

Chapter: 10 Gangsta

"Nigga, what's good? When we making that move for Kozlov?" Trill asked.

"Yeah, we have to go to New York next week to handle

that for Kozlov. He's got a dude who's gonna meet us to grab the merch," I told them, and he nodded.

We were sitting at our spot, which was a small apartment on the west side of the Chicago. This was where we met up to split the money from our heists. I hadn't been out of the motel room in two days, and quite frankly, I was getting tired of the bitch. Nah, let me stop lying. I liked her thick ass.

"So, when you gon' let shawty go, nigga? I'm tryna figure out why the fuck you still holding on to her," Trill asked.

"Nigga, it ain't for you to figure out. I'm gon' let her go, nigga, damn," I snapped.

Trill and Menace started laughing at me. I really didn't want to tell them that I was required to kill her, but I wasn't going to. I liked her. I was gonna have to deal with Kozlov my way, and that's gonna be one mission we would have to take as a loss. My whole game plan had switched up. I was gonna kill her to make Finesse sick with grief, but nah, snatching his bitch and making her mine was gonna be a better one.

"When?"

"When I feel like it, but fuck all of that. We partying tonight or what?" I switched the subject.

Me and my niggas we did the club shit heavy. We wanted these niggas in the city to see who the fuck we were and how we got down.

"Nah, I'm caking it tonight. Me and Fallon supposed to go out," Menace replied, and I chuckled.

"Sucka ass nigga," I retorted, and he stuck up his middle finger.

"Nah, I'm trying to get up with shawty ass tonight, the one who sister you stole," Trill joked, and I shook my head at these niggas. They were lame as fuck.

"Fuck y'all niggas then. I'm gon' get me a bottle and turn up by my fucking self." I shrugged.

Me and my niggas finished chopping it up, and then we all went our separate ways. I drove to my crib and called shawty to come and meet me before I went in the crib and placed my money in the safe. I took out the ten bands I had to give shawty and waited for her in my car.

She pulled up about fifteen minutes later and hopped out her car in some tight ass red pants and a black leather coat. Shawty was all smiles as she sashayed to my car. I rolled down the window and handed her the stack.

'Thanks for that, shawty."

"Anything for you, daddy." Dyna smiled at me.

Dyna had helped me with the robbery. We had a lil something going on a while back, but I couldn't fuck with her like that because she was a sneaky bitch. I always kept her in my pocket because she was a hustling ass bitch, and bitches like that knew how to get down for some paper. Bitches like her wouldn't hesitate to do anything for that almighty dollar.

"Aight, so what's the word? That nigga got any clue?" I asked, fishing for information on Finesse.

"Hell no. He's going about business as usual. Shit, I don't even think he cares that much about her. You know he fucks with this chick named Kari, so he's been with her most of the time." She shrugged, and I only nodded.

I actually knew all I needed to know about the nigga Finesse. I just wanted to see what she knew.

"Yeah, the nigga a true fuck boy, but hit me later on or something. We can make something shake." I winked my eye at her, and she backed away from my car.

"Okay, baby." She smiled.

I peeled away and headed back to the motel I had shawty staying in.

It took me about thirty minutes to make to it back to the other side of the city. When I got to the motel room, shawty was sitting on the bed watching television. Her eyes were bloodshot red, and I could tell she had been crying again. I hated a weak bitch. I chuckled as I placed the bag with my fifth of Hennessey in it on top of the dresser. I took out my Back woods and my 3/5 of loud.

"What's good, shawty," I spoke to her as I untied her wrist from the bedpost and took the gag out of her mouth.

"Hey," she said in a low tone. "You aight?"

"Yes," she replied nonchalantly.

I guessed she wasn't in a talkative mood like she was yesterday. That was cool too. I was letting her ass go tomorrow. I ain't have time to keep babysitting this bitch. This nigga Finesse wasn't about to pay the ransom, and I damn sure wasn't about to hold on to her ass. I had shit to do.

"You hungry?" I asked. "No."

She shook her head, and I decided to leave her the fuck alone. I grabbed my weed off the dresser and sat down in the chair, rolled me a blunt, and then poured myself a shot from my fifth. I was about to get fucked up and fall into my zone. It had been a while since I had a fucking drink. When I was making moves, I liked to be on my P's and Q's at all times. But, tonight, I was letting go. Shit, I needed to unwind.

"Can I have some of that?" she asked. I raised my eyebrow.

"Some of what?"

"The drink. I need a drink badly right now."

Her voice was laced with sadness, and I felt bad as fuck for a minute. I poured her a shot into one of the plastic cups and held it out for her to grab it. She walked over, grabbed the cup out of my hand, and downed it in one gulp.

"Damn, ma. That shit ain't burn ya chest?" I laughed, and she smiled. I was waiting for her to release a smile.

"Nah, it didn't. I'm a drinker. I just don't drink dark liquor. I'm a tequila girl, but anything would do right now." She sighed and then walked back over to the bed.

"What's on ya mind, ma? You ain't talking to a nigga tonight?" I asked as I inhaled the blunt.

"You talking a lot tonight. What's got you in a good mood?" she asked.

"Shit, I'm cool. I'm always cool."

"No, you're an asshole who seems to be a little bipolar." I frowned. "Don't insult me, shawty," I snapped.

"I'm sorry," she whispered and burst into tears.

"Damn, why the fuck you keep crying? Am I abusing you in this muthafucka or something? Am I'm not feeding you? What the fuck, bro? I can't take that crying shit," I snapped on her ass. The shit irritated me to no end.

"I'm sorry, I really am. I just can't help it, okay!" she argued, and I exhaled. I inhaled even harder because she was now blowing me.

"Can I hit that?' she asked, wiping her tears with the back of her hands. "The blunt?" I questioned.

"Yes."

"Damn, you smoke weed too, huh?"

"No, but I wanna try it. I just need to take my mind off some shit for a while."

"Well, shit, if its gon' make you stop crying and shit, then hell yeah, you can hit this muthafucka," I announced then got up and gave her the blunt.

She happily accepted, and when she pulled on it, she started coughing loudly. I burst into laughter as I watched her chocolate skin turn purple.

"Slow down, ma, that ain't no Reggie. That's that good shit," I joked and took my blunt back from her. I sat down on the bed next to her and looked at her.

"Look and learn, Ma." I inhaled the blunt slowly and held the smoke in my mouth.

As I slowly released it, I blew the smoke in her face. Her eyes were on me the entire time. When I handed her the blunt back, she looked skeptical.

"Okay, I want you to hit that muthafucka again," I told her, and she did what I said. This time, she didn't start coughing. She held that shit in like a G.

"Yeah, you hitting that bitch like a G, that's how you do that shit, ma." I smirked, and she laughed.

We got high as fuck as we passed the blunt back and forth between each other. We sipped on the Hennessey as we watched the Avenger's movie on TNT and zoned out.

"Do you have a girl?" she asked out the blue.

I turned to look at her. "Huh? Whatchu mean?"

"I'm just asking. You've been here with me the last five

days, and today makes day six. I'm just wondering if you have a woman at home who is at least worried about you?"

"Nah, ma. I'm a single man."

"I can see why," she said, and I laughed. I swear she popped a lot of shit.

"And why is that?"

"You're an asshole, you're heartless, and you're mean, so I can see how you're single."

"Nah, that ain't why I'm single. Shit, what's love? The shit is just a four-letter word. Imma young, rich, nigga making moves out here. I ain't got time for that shit. Love is for lames. These hoes will make you think you in love then, boom, shit is over. Those the type of hoes who will set they mammy up for a quick buck. Shidddd, never will a G be caught slipping like that. The only bitch I love is Nina, that's my nine. She's loyal, and she ain't never left a nigga's side."

"I hear whatchu saying, so yeah, love might not be for you. No woman wants to put up with that. Love isn't for lames, love just isn't for the weak. You gotta be a strong individual to deal with the things that come with it. Ya nine won't keep you warm at night, ya nine won't have dinner on the table when you get home, and ya nine damn sure won't suck your dick when you need it. That's the difference. Hey, let's be honest, though. You might be fucking with the wrong chicks. Believe me, that love hit different when its real," she spoke, and I heard every word she said.

"Man, fuck these hoes. I'm trying to get money out here." I shrugged, and she laughed

"See what I mean? Crazy and heartless, and as crazy as it may sound, it's attractive to me. And I know damn well I shouldn't be attracted to you. It's all weird to me," she said, throwing me for a loop.

I didn't expect her to say that shit to me. It must be the

Henny that got her talking crazy.

"You're attracted to me because I'm a good-looking nigga, no matter how mean you think I am," I said, and we both laughed.

Then an awkward silence filled the air.

"You're alright. Now, you ain't no GQ model or nothing like that." "Shit, yo ass ugly as fuck, so whatchu saying? Ole black ass," I

retorted with a laugh, and she got quiet.

"Don't get quiet on me now. What's that shit you was popping?" I said.

"I don't joke about my skin complexion. It took me a long time to embrace the beauty of my dark complexion," she stated in a serious tone.

I felt bad as fuck. I hurt her feelings, and I didn't mean to. It was crazy because I didn't know how to say the words, I'm sorry.

"My bad, shawty. I thought we were cracking on each other. I ain't mean to come off like that to you," I apologized in my own way.

"It's okay." She shrugged and took another sip of her drink. "Why do they call you Gangsta?"

"Because I am what I am. I'm a Gangsta, baby." I smirked

"Where did your momma get the name Aspen from?" I asked.

"From my daddy. He's a preacher, but his name is Denver, so she thought it would be a clever idea to name us countries and cities and shit. I don't know. Shit, my momma is weird like that. You got any siblings?" she asked me.

"Yeah, two little sisters." "Oh, okay. That's dope."

"How did you end up with a fuck nigga like Finesse?"

"Ummm, I met Finesse my first year in college. I was going to Loyola University and working at Starbucks. He use to hang around my school, and one day he saw me at work and asked me out. I took him up on his offer, and we've been working through hell and hot water ever since."

"Oh, some love at first sight shit, huh?' I chuckled.

"Nah, not really. More so, some young, dumb, and intrigued by a drug dealer type of shit."

"Damn, that's where these hoes go wrong. Too busy looking at the glitz and glamour, and not enough of the shit going on around them.

"I don't need to be disciplined about the choices I made. I beat myself up every day about that shit. I can't stand what he's put me through."

"You're an adult. You can make the choice to walk the fuck away. I never got that shit with women. Why is it so hard to walk away from a nigga who treated them like shit?"

"You must know somebody who has been hurt before, 'cause you sound bitter," she said.

My moms popped up in my mind, but I didn't say anything. "And it's not always easy to walk away. Things take time." "Shit, I see."

Me and Aspen talked about everything under the sun, until we both ended up dozing off in the bed. I woke up to her head on my chest. I was startled at first, but her skin actually felt good touching mine. I moved her gently off me and grabbed my phone. I checked the time, and it was 6:00 in the morning. I had given her my big t-shirt to put on when she was only clad in the towel, and I knew I couldn't let her go, dressed in only that. So, I grabbed my car keys and walked out the door. There was a 24-hour Walmart in Calumet City. I hopped in my ride and went toward it.

Once inside, I went to the women's department and

found her a jogging suit along with some panties and a bra. I didn't even know if I got the right size or not. I was going strictly off eyesight.

When I made it back to the room, she was still sleeping, and I nudged her awake.

"Aye."

Her eyes instantly popped open.

"Huh? What's wrong?" She sat up in a hurry. "Nothing, ma, get dressed. You about to go home."

I smiled and handed her the Walmart bag. She got up and went in the washroom while I collected all of my shit from around the room and waited for her to emerge. She came out of the bathroom fully dressed, and even though the jogging suit was hugging the shit out of her curves, it still fit her.

"I guess I did good with the sizes, huh?"

"You did. The bra is a little tight, but I can manage." She smirked. "Aight, ma. Let's roll," I told her and led the way out of the motel

room.

We hopped in my ride, and I peeled off. The ride was quiet as we both were lost in our thoughts.

"You know I can't drop you off at your crib, right?" I looked at her, and she smirked.

"I know. Just drop me off down the street from the massage parlor. It's not open right now, but there is a payphone that actually still works on the corner right there. I can call someone there," she said.

It took us about thirty minutes to pull up down the street from the massage parlor. I looked at her, and she exhaled deeply. I didn't know what to say to her ass, I actually didn't feel comfortable letting her leave, but then again, I was confident that she wouldn't open her mouth to the police and say shit about me.

"I just wanna say thank you. Thank you for letting me go, thank you for letting live," she stated and kissed my cheek then got out of the car. I didn't reply as I pulled away.

As I drove to my crib, I hoped like hell I made the right decision and this shit wouldn't come back and bite me in the ass for letting her live. I knew she was loved by her people, and she was innocent in my beef with Finesse. I pulled out my cell and called Kozlov.

"My Young Gangsta. Top of the morning to you." "I let her go," I confessed, and he got quiet.

"We need to meet, and ASAP. I'm sending the jet. I'll text you with the details," he spat.

I knew Kozlov was gonna feel some type of way about what I did, but fuck him.

Chapter: 11 Asia

"Bitchhhhhhhhhhhh," I sang out as I threw my arms around Aspen's neck, for the fifth time.

I had missed my fucking bug ass sister so much.

"You're hurting my neck, A!" She giggled, but I didn't care. I missed her so much.

We were at her and Finesse's crib, and she was clad in her pajamas. I could tell she had just gotten out of the shower. She was all smiles, and I was glad she wasn't hurt.

"Bitch, so what happened? The nigga just let you go? Who the fuck was he?" I rattled off.

"Girl, I don't know. He kept his face covered the entire time. He barely said a word to me. He fed me, but that was it. Then, out of the blue, he threw me in his trunk and dropped me off in front of the massage parlor. I couldn't do anything but cry and thank God he spared my life," she said as tears formed in her eyes.

"Damn, sis, I'm so fucking happy right now. I'm so fucking happy," Ru said and let tears fall from her eyes.

"Bae, so that's it? The nigga ain't say shit? He just let you go, huh?" Finesse asked, looking skeptical.

"He did. He said something about you saying you weren't gonna pay the ransom. He told me you said to go ahead and kill me," she spat.

I looked at Finesse bitch ass. I just knew he ain't say no fucked-up shit like that.

"Man, I ain't tell that nigga no shit like that. I told his ass five mill was a lot of money, and he had to give me time. I had to get that paper up. I ain't have all that shit on me at once," Finesse argued.

"Well, I don't care, bae. I'm just glad to be home," Aspen said.

"I'm about to cook you some breakfast, sis," Ru said and went in the kitchen. We had taken over their house like it was ours.

"I missed you so much, bae."

Finesse kissed her, and I wanted to throw up in my mouth. With his phony ass. I wanted to tell Aspen about Finesse and his bitch so fucking bad, but I figured I'd wait until she was settled in to tell her. His bitch ass wasn't about to get away with that shit.

"I hope you were a good boy while I was gone," Aspen said, and I started coughing.

"Bullshit!" I coughed into my hand, and Finesse glared at me.

"Bae, you already know you're all I want," he said, and she was smiling all giddy and shit.

I really didn't even wanna break her heart.

"AP! Come here for a minute," Ru called Aspen by her nick name. Aspen pulled away from Finesse and walked back into the kitchen with

Aruba. It was only me and Finesse in the living room. "Aye, man, can we keep this shit between us?" he said.

"Ummm, that's my sister. I don't think I could do that," I told him. "You can do it if you want to. But yo, check this shit out. I'll up your pay at the massage parlor. I promise you I ain't even messing with ole girl no more. That's been dead. I swear," he pleaded, and I eyed him.

"Aight, Finesse, I'll keep yo' secret. But fuck with my sister, and I'm gonna fuck you up! I swear," I added.

Finesse smiled while nodding his head. He thought I was playing, but I was dead ass serious. He didn't want this smoke at all. I walked into the kitchen with my sisters and I sat down at the island.

Aspen looked so happy, and I was glad she was back home. My cell vibrated, and it was a text message from Trill. This was the first time he had contacted me since the hospital.

T: what's good wit yo sexy ass Me: Lol! Hey Trill!

T: I wanna see you Me: when???

T: Right now!

Me: Lol! Not today my sister is home. So, I'm chilling. But tomorrow after class, I got you!

T: Oh word! That's what's up! Aight chill with yo peoples, and I'm expecting to hear from you tomorrow. Don't make me come and find you Lips

I giggled when I read that last part. I liked the nick name he gave me.

He was obsessed with my big, soup cooler ass lips. Most of the time they drove niggas crazy, and the thangs that I could do with them.

"Bitch whatchu laughing at?" Ru asked, turning her attention to me. "Girl, nothing. Just this dude texting me." I giggled again.

"Oh shit, who is it now?" Aspen said.

"Oh, here you go with that smart-ass mouth, Aspen." I rolled my eyes at her.

"I'm just saying, you know you keep you a new one on deck."

We all laughed because the shit was true. I switched up niggas like I switched up panties.

"Well, I have an announcement, guys. I got the job at the county that I had applied for!" Aruba said excitedly.

"Awww shit! That's what's up, sis!" I squealed and gave her a hug. Aruba had applied for a position at the Cook County jail to be a CO.

She'd been waiting on that call for a minute now. "Congratulations, baby."

We all hugged. I was proud of Ru for getting out of the damn massage parlor. Shit, we all needed to move around, but I knew Aspen was gonna stay because of Finesse bitch ass.

Aruba threw down in the kitchen, and we had a big ass breakfast. We sat around and ate like a family without Finesse clown ass. Then we went to see our parents. I was surprised that Aspen wanted to see them. Me and Ru never told them that Aspen was missing. We told them that she and Finesse were out of town on a vacation, and she couldn't answer her phone because she didn't have any service.

Today was a good day, and I glad my sister was back. Things could finally go back to normal.

"CLASS, the final paper will be due next Tuesday. This is college, it's no do overs. Take a look at your test and see the things that you've done wrong and correct them. And with that said, everyone, have a great day," Professor Garrett spoke.

I looked down at my test and then back up at him. I couldn't believe this shit. He was gonna stop me from getting my bachelor's. Every time I looked up, it was something with him. I had a D on my test. This shit wasn't right. I answered all the questions properly, so I couldn't understand what the fuck I did wrong. I didn't deserve this grade.

Once half of the class left, I walked up to him. He turned to me and smiled.

"How can I help you, Ms. Walters?"

"I have some questions about my test. Why did I receive a D?" "Because you didn't explain the theory of the criminal behavior, which

was the basis of the exam."

"But, I did. If it wasn't to your liking, that's one thing, but to give me a D as if I didn't explain it at all is messed up."

I expressed myself openly to whoever and didn't bite my tongue. I was pissed because I got all D's in his class, and it was fucking with my grades.

"Ms. Walters, look over the exam, and hopefully it will help you improve. Try to use your resources for the paper that's due next Tuesday. Now, if there isn't anything else, please have a great day," he stated and turned his back to me. I was outdone by his smug ass.

I wanted to say something smart, but I decided to let it go. His ole creep ass. I walked out of the school pissed the fuck off. I hopped in my ride, and as I drove, my cell chimed. I picked it up once I was at a stop light and checked to see who it was. It was Rico. I smiled when I saw his name. He was finally home from the hospital, but he wasn't back in school yet.

Rico: You don't fuck with me no more big head. Me: Heyyyy Brother!

Rico: What's up? You good?

Me: Yup! I'm about to come and see you right now!

After texting Rico, I did a U-turn and headed for his crib.

When I pulled up, there were two cars sitting in the driveway, which was odd because his moms didn't drive. I hopped out my ride and made my way to the front door. After I knocked heavily on the door, it came open.

"Hey, Mrs. Porter." I hugged Rico's mom then she stepped to the side and allowed me in.

"Rico is in the den. That's been his home since he's been released from the hospital." She smiled, and I nodded.

I knew exactly where the den was because that's where we studied at majority of the time if it wasn't at the library.

I walked into the den, and he was sitting on the couch playing the video game with Trill beside him. They both looked up at me and smiled.

"Hey, bro." I went over and hugged Rico. "Hey, Trill," I spoke.

"What's up, Lips? How you doing?"

"I'm good. What's good though, bro? How you been feeling?" I turned my attention to Rico.

"I'm maintaining, sis. I'm healing, so that's a good thing. You ain't hit a nigga up lately, so I was just trying to see how you been."

"Garrett is working my fucking nerves, bro." I scoffed, and Trill looked at me funny.

"Who the fuck is Garrett?" Trill barked.

Rico and I burst into laughter. The jealousy stunt was cute on him. "Boy, my fucking professor!" I screeched.

"Aight, 'cause I was about to say, don't get fucked up, Lips," he snarled.

I thought that was some funny ass shit. This nigga was touched in the head for real.

"Baby, chill out. You know I don't want nobody but you,"

I joked in a sexy ass voice.

"You playing, but I'm dead ass serious," he shot back.

"Look, bro, wait ya fucking turn. I know you feeling Asia and all, but that's my homie, and I'm tryna chill with her," Rico intervened.

We both were shocked at his tone of voice. I didn't say shit, and neither did Trill.

Eventually Trill got up and said he had to handle some business, so I kicked it with Rico for about two hours. We discussed school, his lil bitch he was chilling with, and how he felt when he got shot.

When I was done chilling with him, his mom walked me to the door. As I left their house, I spotted Trill sitting on top of his car talking to two guys. One was buff as hell, and the other one had some long dreadlocks. They all locked at me, and I felt awkward. I power walked to my car, which was sitting on the street. Before I could get all the way there, Trill called my name.

"Aye, Lips."

I looked behind me, and he was already walking my way. I stopped and leaned on the hood of my car.

"What's up?"

"You keep tryna curve me? What? You don't like a nigga or something?" he asked.

"Yeah, I do."

"Then, why you be acting like that? What's up with you?"

"I have a lot of shit going on right now in my life. That's all, I don't be meaning it that way."

"I thought you said after school we were gonna chill out? What happened to that shit?"

"I did say that, but as you can see, I came over to chill with Rico. He's my friend, and I haven't seen him since he was in the hospital," I explained.

"Aight, I hear that, Lips, but I'm talking about now. I wanna chill, so what's up?"

I exhaled and pondered it for a minute. I really didn't have a clue as to why I was curving Trill.

"Okay. Let me go change clothes, and we can go out or something." "Nah, you coming to my crib. Text me when you're done getting ready

and shit, and I'll send you my address," he stated.

I nodded and opened my car door, and then he closed it right back. "Whatchu doing?" I eyed him.

"Give me a fucking kiss before you just hop in yo shit like that," he snapped.

I laughed. This nigga had a lot of balls. I leaned in and kissed his lips slowly. I don't know why the hell I did, but I did.

"Aight, that's more like it. Now hurry yo ass up. Daddy missed you."

He smacked my ass, and I hopped in my car. I drove home with a smile on my face the entire time. Trill was something else with his bluntness. He just did something to me with his boss ass nature. I wasn't used to dudes demanding shit from me.

Chapter: 12 Trill

This morning, I woke up with a bad ass attitude. I wasn't the type of nigga who was used to waiting on bitches hand and foot, and this bitch, Asia, was trying me. We were supposed

to get up last night, but she played a nigga to the left. She didn't respond to any of my text messages, nor did she answer any of my phone calls.

I thought she was rocking with a nigga, but I guess not. I was horny as fuck. Shit, I ain't had no pussy, and she had me gone off that one time I smashed. I wasn't about to sit back and act like some thirsty ass nigga who couldn't get no bitch. Fuck her.

I walked into my kitchen and I threw the lobster tails and shit I had ordered into the garbage. I didn't even put the shit in the fridge last night when I figured she was playing me. Me being me, ordered a bunch of food, bought some Moet, and tried to set the mood. But, instead, I was shitted on yet again by her ass. Instead of wilding out, I just got blunted out and fell asleep.

I walked into my bathroom and turned on the shower. In two days, me and the crew had to go to New York for a job, so I needed to get my head tighter. I couldn't get this chick off my mind, though. It was something about her ass.

After showering, I got dressed and was out the door. Today, I had plans. I was looking at some properties, so I could open a business or two. I needed to clean up some of this money.

My cell chimed as I drove through the hoods. I picked my

cell out of the cup holder, and it was Nika calling me. I answered before it went to voicemail.

"Whaddup, Nika?"

"Hey, Trill, are you busy right now?" she asked.

"Yeah and no. What's up? You good?" I asked.

"No, my fucking car won't start, and my mother is gone way out in the 'burbs. I need to get to school. Today is my first day, and I don't wanna be late for my first class." She sounded frustrated.

"What school you at?"

"I just started at Loyola," she spoke, and I chuckled.

How fucking ironic was it that she went to the same school that Asia and Rico attend.

"Aight, I'll be there in like twenty minutes. Be outside, Nika. I got some shit I gotta handle today, and I can't be late," I instructed her and then hung up the phone.

When I pulled in front of her house, I was surprised that she was sitting on her porch. I could never wife Nika's ass up because she was too much of a hoe, but I couldn't help but admire her banging ass body.

She sashayed to the car, and I noticed her fat ass in them black leggings. Staring at her had my dick hard and ready. I considered telling her let's go inside for a minute, so she could let me hit, but I had to stay focused. She got in the car and looked over at me with a smile.

"What's up?"

"Hey, baby." She smirked.

I started my ignition and peeled away. I headed for Lake Shore Drive and started my trek to the fucking Northside. As we drove, I bumped Lil Wayne's The Carter 5 album. I looked over at Nika, and she was staring out the window like she had a lot of shit on her mind.

"What's up? You aight?"

"Nah, not really, but it ain't shit I can't handle."

"Oh, aight. Man, I didn't know your ass went to school," I told her because I honestly didn't know. I just thought she was some dumb ass hood rat,

"Yeah, I'm going for physiology. I was going to DePaul, but I transferred because Loyola has better academics."

"Oh shit, okay, ma. I like that. I just never knew that shit."

There's a lot about me that you don't know, Trill, and that's because you never tried to get to know me."

"You right about that. I see no lies, ma. It was never intentional, though. I be having a lot of shit going on, so I kept it moving."

"I get it, but thank you for doing this for me," she said, and I nodded.

I turned my music back up and drove down the highway. We pulled up to her school forty-five minutes later due to the traffic.

"Thank you so much, baby, I really appreciate it." She kissed me on the cheek and got out of the car.

She started walking off, and I got out the car and called her name. "Nika! Nika!" I shouted out. She turned around and walked back over

to the car.

"Here, go and get your car fixed." I went into my pocket and peeled off eight one hundred-dollar bills.

"Can I get a couple of dollars?" a voice said from behind me.

It was Asia walking past with some chick. She held a smirk on her face like shit was sweet. Man, fuck her.

"I ain't got it," I told her, and Nika smiled.

She thought she had one up on Asia, but I wasn't thinking about either one of them hoes.

"Thank you, baby," Nika squealed, I guess trying to make Asia jealous.

Asia couldn't take her eyes off me while she walked past laughing. Nika kissed me again, this time on the lips, and I was caught off fucking guard. I didn't like that shit at all. She knew I didn't kiss her ass in the fucking mouth. I didn't say shit because I wanted to make Asia jealous. Once Asia was past us, I grabbed Nika by the back of her head. Then got the fuck out of there.

I had moves to make, and I didn't have time for the goofy shit today.

While riding, my phone vibrated in my lap.

Lips: Oh, really my nigga?

Me: Lol

Lips: That bitch basic anyway Me: Looks better than you Lips: Nigga you wish

Me: Lol

Lips: You tricking off now. Shit, next time I'll charge you for the pussy

Me: Aight I got yo $50 holla at me

Lips: Fuck your nigga

I didn't respond to Asia's last text message. I wasn't in the mood to be going back and forth with her ass. She was in her feelings about seeing me pull up with Nika, but she didn't give a fuck when she shitted on me. I continued my day without thinking about Asia or Nika.

☙

INHALING THE KUSH, my mind relaxed as I sat at home chilling. The crib was quiet. I had ordered me some Chinese food, and I was zoned out. I didn't have any bitches around, and frankly, I didn't wanna be bothered with them hoes no way.

As I watched the news, I started to feel my eyelids get heavy. I was tired as fuck. Turning off the television, I stood up and was about to head to my bedroom until knocking at my front door startled me.

I grabbed my banger from underneath the couch and slowly walked to my front door. When I looked through the peephole and saw who was standing on the other side, it caused me to chuckle. I opened the front door and leaned in the door-frame.

"Can I help you?" I smirked, eyeing Asia's pretty chocolate ass.

She brushed past me and entered my apartment without being invited in. She was sporting a trench coat and some black pumps. I closed my front door and looked at her.

"What's good, Lips?"

"You got my fifty dollars?" she asked me, and I laughed. "I ain't got it right now."

"Well, that's fine. I do freebies sometimes," she stated and opened her trench coat.

Asia was sporting a red lace bra and some red panties. The red looked good as fuck on her chocolate ass skin. I pulled her close to me and wrapped my hands around my waist. She smelled so fucking good. I didn't know what the fuck Asia was doing to me, but, her chocolate ass was driving me crazy.

"Whatchu tryna do? You tryna give me some of that pussy?" I whispered in a husky tone

"Like I said, you got my money?" She looked at me with a

smirk on her face, and I chuckled.

"What about the freebies you said you do?" I asked.

She smiled, dropped to her knees, and pulled my dick out. Slowly, she sucked the head, and I closed my eyes as I relished the way she was making me feel. Her lips were juicy as hell, and her mouth was warm and inviting.

"Damn, Lips," I said as my breathing got shallow.

It was enough of the dick sucking; I was ready to feel them walls. I pulled her up and picked her up bridal style then carried her to my bedroom.

Me and Lips fucked for about two hours, and it was better than the first time I sexed her ass in the car. Now we lay in the bed smoking a blunt. It was quiet, and we both were lost in our thoughts.

"Who was that? Ya girlfriend?" she asked me as she inhaled the blunt.

"Nah."

"Well, who was she?" "A friend."

"A friend I should be worried about?" "Whatchu gonna be worried about her for?"

"I'm just saying. I don't need no fucking issues with yo bitches."

"You the bitch I'm digging on right now, so no worries." She glared at me after I said that, and I laughed.

"Don't play with me, Trill. Call me another bitch and see what happens."

"My bad, Lips. I'm just bullshittin' but nah, shorty ain't shit but a friend. We rock from time to time, but in your own words, I belong to no one."

"Well, that dick belongs to me, so we gonna get that understood right now."

"Is that so?" I smirked.

"Hell yeah, that's so. You can't be fucking me like that and not expect for me to stalk yo ass, nigga," she stated.

I touched her cheek. She was so damn pretty to me.

"When you get your hair done like that? I like that shit," I said, acknowledging the long ass weave she now had. It was different from the short hair she had sported before.

"Got it done today when I left school. I'm glad you like it, and I'm also glad you noticed it."

"Believe me, I notice everything about you, Lips," I told her, and she blushed.

"Is that so?" she shot back

"Hell yeah. Now lemme get a kiss." She leaned in and gently kissed me.

I was feeling Lips to the fullest. I didn't know where this shit was headed, but I was willing to see how far it would go. I wasn't no relationship type of nigga, but I wouldn't hesitate to go into one with her. She had a good head on shoulders, she was a freak, and she was low key gangsta. Just my type of woman.

Chapter: 13 Aspen

"Ohhh shit, bae! Yessss baby! Yessss," I screamed as Finesse stroked me gently from the back.

Ever since I've been back home, Finesse had been fucking

me like it was going on of style. He was waiting on me hand and foot; any and everything I wanted, he gave it to me. He was so sweet and gentle with me over the last few weeks, and it was surprising.

I hadn't been worried about him staying out all night, and I wasn't worried about the chick Kari calling his phone all night. Things had been good.

"Get on top and ride this dick," he demanded, and I happily obliged.

He flipped on his back, and I climbed on top of him. I slowly eased down on his dick. He filled me up, and I started move back and forth on top of him. Finesse cupped my breasts and played with my nipples using his thumbs. Closing my eyes, I tried to stay focused, but Gangsta's face popped in my mind. Picturing his thick body and full lips, I bucked my hips harder.

"OOohhhh shit," I whispered as I thought about it being Gangsta's dick in me instead of Finesse.

His deep voice replayed in my mind, and the way he licked his luscious lips when he talked to me had me riding Finesse's dick even harder.

"OOohhhh, shit!" I moaned as I felt my nut build up.

"Yes, bae, ride daddy's dick." Finesse groaned, but I tuned him out.

I didn't give a fuck what he was saying. All I could see was Gangsta in my mind, all I could see was Gangsta fucking me like only a thug could.

"OOohhhh, Gangsta!" I screamed as I came all over Finesse dick.

Whap!

I opened my eyes, and tears raced to the forefront as the sting of Finesse back hand caught me off guard. I was so in the moment that I finally realized what I did. I called him another man's name.

"Bitch get the fuck off me," he spat and pushed me off of him.

I fell off the bed and sat on the floor looking stupid. I didn't know what the fuck to say. I had just fucked up.

"Bitch, did you just call me another nigga's name while you was riding my dick?" he barked.

"No... No... I..." I stuttered.

I couldn't get the words out. I was scared, and I didn't even wanna attempt to say sorry because I knew I was guilty.

"You what, bitch?" Finesse barked and walked around to the side of the bed where I was sitting.

He grabbed my braids and dragged me toward the bathroom

"Finesse! What are you doing?! Let me fucking go! Let me fucking!" I screamed as his grip got tighter and tighter on my hair. I had just gotten these braids and they were tight as hell.

"Bitch you been fucking someone else? Who the fuck is Gangsta?

Who the fuck you been fucking, bitch?" he growled.

He was heated, and I was scared.

"No one! I ain't been fucking nobody, Finesse! I fucking swear!" I cried, but he wasn't hearing me.

"Bitch, you're lying! Wash yo stank ass pussy and yo stank ass mouth out! Now! Before I beat yo ass in this bitch!" he growled.

I slowly got off the floor walked to the sink. As I stared in the mirror, my body trembled with fear at the thought of Finesse wilding out and hurting me some more.

"Wash yo' mouth out with soap, bitch, and I'm not playing," he threatened.

I looked at his ass like he was crazy. I wasn't about to put no soap in my mouth. Fuck that.

"I'm not doing that, Finesse. I said I was sorry," I spat, and he glared at

me.

Instead of going back and forth with him, I walked ran some bath

water and got in the tub as tears escaped from my eyes. Finesse stared at me in the mirror the entire time, and I closed my eyes because I couldn't even look at him. I was too fucking embarrassed by what I did.

"Yo, fuck this, and fuck you. I'm out this bitch!" he barked, and I shook my head.

I knew that was coming next. I watched him in the bathroom mirror as he walked away. Moments later, I heard the front door slam, and I broke down crying.

I didn't know what the fuck was wrong with me; I shouldn't even be thinking about Gangsta at a time like that, but I was. Honestly, I couldn't get his ass off my mind. The more

I tried not to think about him, the more I thought about him.

Those five days with him, made me see him in a different light. He was a gentle giant who I wanted to know on a much more personal level. He had kidnapped me, but I still didn't wanna see any harm come to him. That's why I never revealed that I knew who he was.

I washed up, got out of the tub, and climbed in my bed. I was mad that Finesse left, but I had nobody to blame but myself. Finesse probably ran back to the arms of Kari, and at this point in my life, I didn't care. Gangsta floating through my thoughts was enough for me.

♡

"HEY, SIS, YOU OKAY?" Ru asked we sipped on Frappes from McDonald's.

I was unusually quiet today. It had been two days since the incident with Finesse, and he hadn't answered any of my calls. He hadn't come home either. Quite frankly, I was over the bullshit with his ass.

"I'm good, girl, just some shit on my mind. How you been, though?" I asked.

"I'm chilling. I start at the county next week, but you know with me having a new job and all, I'm not gonna be able to work like I want to. I mean, I can still help out from time to time."

"No, Ru, it's fine. You handle all your shit. I know for a fact that we'll be able to handle this place with you gone," I assured her.

"I know y'all will, but seriously though. Aspen, what's wrong?" she asked me again, and I let out a deep sigh.

"Girl, me and Finesse got into a fight two days ago, and he

hasn't been home, nor is he answering his phone. I know deep down inside he's with ole girl." I spoke how I felt, and I knew Ru would understand, unlike Asia, who was the more go beat his ass type of chick.

"Girl I didn't wanna tell you because Asia begged me not to. She said it would be too much for you when you came home, but one day when you were missing, me and Asia went to y'all house to talk to Finesse and see what he was doing about your situation, and a bitch was in y'all crib. She was a light skinned chick with a fake ass booty." She scoffed, and my mouth dropped open.

"Why wouldn't y'all tell me that shit?" I snapped

"Because we didn't wanna break your heart sis, You had just gotten home and I knew it wouldn't be too much for you"

"Y'all don't know what would've been too much instead of me walking around looking fucking stupid while a whole bitch was in my crib," I argued back.

"Aspen, let's keep it real. You've been stupid over Finesse for a long fucking time. If we would have told you right then and there, would you have done anything? You probably wouldn't have even left him."

"Again, you don't know what I would've done had I been informed." I rolled my eyes, but she was right. I let Finesse run me into the ground.

"You know what, sis? I'm sorry, alright? We were wrong. Regardless of how we felt, we should've told you because I realized when you were gone that life is too short, and I prayed every single day for God to bring you back," she apologized.

I only nodded my head. I didn't have much to say. They were wrong, period. Whether I chose to say with Finesse or not was my business. They still should've told me simply because I was their sister.

"It's all good," I dryly replied and finished focusing on my task at hand.

I didn't have anything else to say on the matter. I would handle Finesse when I got home. The nerve of him to bring that bitch into my house. I kept my cool, but on the inside, I was fucking fuming.

As me and Ru let the silence take over, she got up and walked to the back of the massage parlor. I pulled out my cell and dialed up Finesse one more time.

"Yeah?" he answered on the first ring, which shocked the hell outta me because I expected him not to answer.

"Ummm, hey... where are you?" I asked. "Out making moves. What's up?"

"I was calling to check on you, that's it. I miss you, bae. Come home," I told him.

"Yeah? Well, I'll be there later," he spat in a nasty tone.

I exhaled deeply because I didn't wanna do this shit with him "Okay, Finesse. I—"

My sentence was halted when I spotted a black Range Rover pull up in front of the massage parlor. The driver hopped out, he sported a thick ass leather coat with fur on the hood. I could tell it was a Pelle. He had on a pair of wheat Timbs, and his music was blasting. He sat on the hood of the car. I squinted and swallowed hard when I noticed it was Gangsta.

"Lemme call you back, bae," I said and hung the phone up in Finesse face. I instantly got nervous, and I didn't know why.

"Who the hell is blasting that fucking music like that?" Ru said, coming from the back.

"I... I don't know. Let me go and see."

I came from behind the counter and went outside, pretending that I needed to see who it was. When I got outside I walked up on Gangsta, and he was smoking a blunt. He held a smirk on his handsome ass face, and I sort of blushed, but I had to put my game face on. This nigga had a lot of nerve popping up there.

"What the fuck are you doing here?" I asked him and propped my hand on my hip.

"I came to see you, shorty. Why do you think?" He grinned.

"Well, it isn't a good idea to be coming here. This is my job, and this is also the place that my man owns. He wouldn't like it if he popped up, and you were here."

"I just saw that nigga riding around in a Porsche truck with a bitch in his front seat. I had the opportunity to blow his shit loose, but I remained humble. I let his ass live 'cause I ain't wanna break ya heart. It's obvious you still love the fuck nigga, but that's all gonna change once you learn how to open ya mind up for a real nigga." He stared at me intensely, and I lowered my head.

It was crazy how I was just thinking about this man, how I called this man's name out in the midst of making love a couple of nights ago, and now he was in my presence. That had to mean something for us. That had to be fate.

"Well, fuck him and that bitch. I know where I stand with him," I said, trying to save face.

True enough, I was embarrassed as all hell. Finesse made a fool of me daily, but him and his bitch wasn't gonna kill me. I had to shake that nigga, and fast, but honestly, I didn't know how I was gonna live without Finesse. I didn't have a skill. I didn't finish school… I was just nothing.

"I know where you stand too. You gon' be his widow in a couple weeks, so prepare your goodbyes now." He smirked, and I shook my head. "What do you want, Gangsta?" I exhaled deeply, tired of the back and

forth already.

"You can call me Geon. That Gangsta shit is only for these niggas in the streets. Now come and take a ride with me. Before you say no, understand that I know how to kidnap bitches." He laughed, and I pushed him the chest.

"Let me grab my purse and my phone, damn." I playfully rolled my eyes.

I went back inside, and Aruba was standing there with a stupid ass grin on her face.

"Girl, who the fuck is that?" she asked.

"None of ya business. Lock up for me, sis, please. I'll give you all the details in the morning."

I kissed her cheek and grabbed my white leather jacket off the coat rack. When I walked back outside, and Gangsta was sitting in his truck waiting for me. Hopping in the truck, I was skeptical, but then again, I wasn't. Finesse was doing him, so why not I have a little fun as well?

Gangsta peeled away from the massage parlor, and I didn't know where he was taking me, but I was excited all the same.

"So, what's good, shorty? Whatchu been doing?" he asked, making casual conversation.

I looked over at his weird ass and laughed.

"Nigga, I've been working. Glad to be back home and not in a motel room."

"Man, look, I apologize about that again. Somehow, I wish you was an ugly bitch, so I wouldn't feel bad, and I also wouldn't be digging you right now."

"Too bad I'm not ugly." We both laughed.

It was awkward for both of us, but I think but I liked his ass. "Where you taking me?"

"Shit I don't know, somewhere." He shrugged, and I didn't

like that. "Ohhh, okay."

"Man, getcho scary ass outta here. You good, Ma. If I wanted to do something to you, I would have. Stop worrying. What I tell you about that worrying shit?" He frowned as he glanced over at me.

"I'm just saying, our history ain't the best, ya know," I replied as he got on the Dan Ryan expressway.

"So, tell me, how was life for you growing up?" he asked. "Heaven and hell." I summed it up in those two words. "Word?"

"Yeah..." My mind drifted off thinking about my past. I had some skeletons too. Some shit I never discussed, and I didn't care to discuss. I figured leaving the past in the past was the best option for me.

"Yeah, mine was just pure hell. Know what I mean?"

"I can tell, with yo' mean ass," I joked.

"I ain't mean, baby. I'm serious. There's a difference." "Yeah, you're right."

When he finally stopped the car, we were in a wooded area. A bunch of trees surrounded us, I was scared because it was almost 7:00 at night. I loosened up when I spotted the parking lot full of cars. Curiosity got the best of me as we hopped out the truck. Gangsta took my hand and led me toward the open field. What I saw when we got to the open field had my mouth hanging the fuck open.

"The fuck? Awww, hell no, nigga. I'm not doing that shit," I screeched, eyeing all the hot air balloons. There were multiple couples getting into the hot air balloons and lifting off into the sky, but I wasn't with that shit.

"Yo crybaby ass. Ma, you gotta be my G-Baby."

"Wait, what? What the hell is your G-Baby first off? And secondly, scary? Hell no, I ain't scary. I'll whup a bitch's ass, but I'm terrified of fucking heights, and I can't help it."

"Well, tonight you gotta thug that shit out. What I tell you about that scary shit? I ain't tryna hear it, and yo ass better not start crying," he scolded me, and I looked at his ass like he was fucking crazy.

"Boy, fuck you," was the only response I had for his ass.

Grabbing my hand, he led me to the lady who was operating the hot air balloon.

"What do a hood nigga like you know about shit like this? This wasn't random, you planned this." I eyed his ass.

"I know a lot, and I also know women like this mushy ass shit." He chuckled.

"What if I wouldn't have come along with you?" I questioned.

"Then I would've gotten one of these hoes I fuck around with to accompany me, but I don't like them like that. You're the only muthafucka that been on my mind since I left you," he admitted, and I swallowed hard.

Finesse was a liar, but Gangsta was bold as fuck by the mouth.

We both got inside, and surprisingly, there was an ice bucket, two glasses, and a bottle of champagne in it. As the balloon ascended into the sky, I couldn't help but look at how pretty the stars were.

"Wow, this is beautiful," I whispered.

Finesse had never done no shit like this for me.

"It is. You're beautiful, though," Gangsta whispered in my ear as he wrapped his arms around my waist from the back.

The hairs on the back of my neck stood up, and I felt funny with him touching me like that. "Thank you."

"Tell me something. You ready to be my G-Baby?" he whispered.

His breath tickled the back of my neck, and he gave me goose bumps.

The way he made me feel was unheard of. "What's your G-Baby?"

"My everything, my rider, my gangsta boo, my lover... Everything that a G needs," he stated, and I chuckled.

"I have a man, Geon, who I happen to love, who you tried to extort money from. You don't even know me well enough to be saying I'm gonna be your G-Baby or whatever."

"I know enough, ma, and I also know when I see something, I want, and I go after it hard as fuck. I'm a lil rough around the edges, but that's what comes with loving a nigga like me. You'll get used to it."

"Oh, you confident. I'm just gon' fuck with you, huh? After you kidnapped me, held me hostage in a filthy ass room, called me multiple bitches, and let's not forget clocking me in the damn head with a fucking gun." I rolled my eyes, and he smirked.

"Why you bringing up old shit, though?" he joked, and we both laughed.

"Nah, but seriously though, this is awkward for me. I like you, you're an interesting person, but I have too much other shit going on with myself, and then there's the thing with Finesse. It's like—"

"Aye, man, look. Stop bringing that nigga up when you with me. I hear whatchu saying, but I don't really hear you, though. Shit gonna happen whether you want it to or not, and believe me, that nigga Finesse is a fucking clown, ma. You gon' learn one day, though," he stated.

Deep down inside, I felt he was right. I couldn't stop thinking about him before tonight, and he popped back up at the massage parlor. It must be meant to be.

"I won't bring him back up, but I also don't want you to keep popping up on me. It's nothing to receive my phone number," I said.

"Well, make sure you leave me those digits." He smirked.

Gangsta held me close to him as we sipped the champagne and looked at the stars. It seemed corny, but it was by far the most beautiful thing I have ever experienced, and that right there was what set him apart from Finesse. I didn't know what was going to happen with me and Gangsta, but I was scared, anxious, and excited to see where the road leads us.

Chapter: 14 Gangsta

'Hi, you have reached Aspen. Unfortunately, I'm busy right now, so leave your name and number, and I'll get back with you later." Aspen's voicemail announced again.

I had been calling her fucking every day. Today made a week since our lil date, and she had been ignoring a nigga ever since I dropped her to her car.

I didn't know what it was about her ass that had a nigga soft as fuck, but I wasn't liking it. This shit wasn't a part of my plans to take down Finesse. I was supposed to kill the fuck nigga, but I couldn't do it because I knew she still called herself in a relationship with the nigga. It was time for her ass to get with the program.

I was pissed off that I couldn't get in touch with her. I wanted to ride to their crib and drag her ass outta that house, but I knew that wasn't my place. I didn't wanna scare her off any more than I had already done.

Knocking on my front door got my attention. I walked to the door and looked through the peephole. It was Dyna. I opened the door and let her come in.

"Hey, babe, I got your food." She handed me the Popeyes bag, and the shit smelled good as hell.

It was crazy how I was able to get Dyna to do any and everything I asked her to.

"Thanks, shorty. What's good, though? You cool?"

"Yeah, I'm fine, babe. They ain't really been fucking with me like that at the job. I think they know something," she said and shrugged.

"Who fucking cares? Fuck them." I grabbed the Popeyes bag and sat down at my dining room table.

"When will you be back?" she asked.

"In a week. I won't be gone long, baby." I smirked at her.

Dyna was a cute chick, loyal to the bone, money driven, and she had some good pussy and bomb ass head, but she just wasn't the chick for me.

"Okay, well don't make it long, baby. I'm gonna miss you."

She came over and kissed me on the cheek. I smacked her on the ass as she walked past me and headed for the door. Before she could open the front door, there was another knock.

"You expecting some company?" she asked.

"Hell naw. Move back, shawty," I instructed her as I grabbed my Glock and headed for the door.

I looked through the peephole, and my heart raced. How the fuck she know where my crib was? I wondered as I opened the door for Aspen. She was standing there smiling, and I mugged her happy ass.

"What the fuck you doing at my crib? And how the fuck you know where I live?" I barked, and the smile dropped from her face.

"I know where you live because you brought me to your house after we left the hot air balloon thing that night. Remember you said you forgot something here and had to stop by. And, secondly, I'm here because I wanted to see you again, but if it's a problem, I can leave," she snapped, and I smirked.

I forgot all about grabbing my shit that night from the crib with her in the car with me. She didn't come inside, but still, that's how she knew where I lived.

"Damn, this how you doing it now, boss lady?" Dyna said.

I could've smacked the shit outta this ditzy ass broad. She had to make her presence known. I didn't understand women for the life of me. I hadn't stuck my dick in Dyna in months, and she was still stuck on a nigga.

"Dyna?" Aspen squinted and frowned.

"Hey, Boss Lady." She chuckled and walked past, but Aspen did some shit that took me by surprise.

She grabbed Dyna's long ponytail and brought her down to the floor in the hallway.

"Bitch! You set me up to get kidnapped! I knew you were a sneaky bitch," Aspen screamed as she threw blows, striking Dyna as hard as she could in her face. I let her get her anger out on Dyna before I broke that shit up.

"Aye! Aye! Cool out, muthafuckas," I shouted as I pulled Aspen off her.

Aspen shook me off her then turned around and slapped the shit out of me. I drew back as if I was gonna hit her because my reflexes made me want to, but I didn't.

"Hit me muthafucka, I dare you!" she snapped, and I smiled. "I see yo' ass ain't that muthafuckin' scary."

"Fuck you, nigga! Yo' psycho ass. I don't know why I brought my stupid ass over here! I'm tired of every fucking body making me out to be some type of fool! Fuck everybody! And, bitch, your weak ass is fucking fired."

She glared at Dyna, who was picking herself up off the porch. She then stormed off and hopped in her car. I shook my head because shit shouldn't have gone down like that. I looked at Dyna and got pissed off all over again.

"Bitch, getcho funky ass off my fucking porch." "Ga—"

"Nah, nah, shut the fuck up. If you would've kept ya mouth closed, yo' shit wouldn't be bleeding right now. That's what yo ass get. You just put me and you on the muthafucking spot. You should've hidden in the back or something until she was gone, but you had to let yourself be known. Now, look. Yo ass looking stupid around this bitch," I barked.

"I'm just gonna leave," she said with her head hung.

"Yeah, you do that," I spat and walked back into my crib, slamming the door in the process.

♡

"AIGHT, so nigga, where you headed to?" Menace asked as he drove from the airport.

Me, Menace, and Trill had just finished a job in New York. We'd been gone for a week, and that score had garnered us a cool two mill each.

"Drop me off at the crib," I instructed him. "Oh, aight."

"Not the one out south, though. The one in the burbs," I explained.

Trill looked at me through the rear-view mirror "Damn, nigga, what warranted the change of scenery?"

"Nothing much. I haven't been out there in a while." I shrugged his question off.

As we rode through the streets of the Chi, Aspen's pretty ass face ran across my mind. She was pissed at me for that lil stint Dyna pulled, and who can blame her? She hadn't answered her phone for me since that day. I needed to see her; I hadn't even fucked her yet, and she made me feeling some type of way. Me and shawty had a connection, and she knew it. All she had to do was comply and become mine, but she was fighting me on this shit.

I was so deep in thought that I hadn't realized we had pulled up to my spot. I couldn't get Lanay off my mind either. I hadn't even bothered to ask Kozlov about her. I didn't believe a word this bitch said out of her mouth. She could be lying about a muthafucking kid that was supposedly mine. I didn't trust that bitch, but the what ifs still lingered in the back of my mind.

Snapping out of my thoughts, I took out the electronic gate opener and open the gate so that Menace could pull up to my crib.

"Bruh, why the fuck is this house so damn big?" Menace scoffed, and I chuckled.

"Nigga, being locked up will make you never want another small, cramped up ass space again," I stated as I hopped out the car.

I dapped then both up, and they pulled off.

I went in my house, deactivated my alarm, and checked every room. I then checked the video tape from the last time I was home, and everything was cool. Sensing that I was straight, I walked through my kitchen and opened the door that led to my garage. In my garage were my play things. I had two Ferraris, a Porsche truck, and my number one girl, my cherry red Lamborghini.

I hopped in my Lamborghini and peeled out. I headed two blocks down from my house and pulled up to the big house on the left-hand side. I parked in front of the door and turned up my radio, blasting it as loud as I could. A particular song happened to be playing, and I laughed at the irony.

She got me speedin' in the fast lane,

Pedal to the floor man, tryna get back to her love, her love Best believe she got that good thing,

She my lil' hood thing, ask around they know us, know us
They know that's my (bust it) baby

Everybody know that's my (bust it) baby Everybody know that's my

I got out my car, grabbing my gun in the process. Then I placed the gun on my lap as I sat on top the hood of the car. I sparked up my blunt and waited for some action. I was about to disturb the peace around this bitch.

About ten minutes later, the front door came flying open, and dressed in her pajamas, Aspen stood wide eyed she tried to figure out what the fuck was going on.

"Nigga, are you fucking crazy?" she screeched and looked around for that bitch ass nigga, Finesse.

"I am, but you know that already." I grinned and inhaled the blunt once more.

"Get away from my house, Geon! What if my man was home?"

"Hell naw! Not until you tell me why the fuck you been ignoring my calls and text messages. And fuck that nigga. You know I want all the smoke with his bitch ass," I barked and glared at her.

"This is becoming a whole other level of stalker shit! I got a man! I mean, that hot air balloon thing you did was nice and all, but this ain't gon' happen with us. You be on some other shit," she stressed.

"Man, shut that shit up." I moved closer to her. "You playing all tough like you all happy in that big house alone because I know that nigga not here. Why the fuck you playing with me? I don't sweat bitches, and you trying me like I'm a lame or something."

"Do you hear your fucking self right now? Nigga, I didn't ask you to sweat me! I couldn't care fucking less right now."

"Yeah, I hear myself. You think I would be here if it wasn't much more to us? We vibe, man, and you know it."

"Listen, I'm confused, okay! I feel things that I shouldn't feel for someone who did something to me. I mean, you kidnapped me, and I shouldn't have fucking feelings toward you. In fact, I should hate you, but I don't. I love a man who I shouldn't love, and I've been dealing with his bullshit for years, and that's fucking with me too! I just wish everybody would stop pressing me so fucking hard! Damn."

I didn't respond. If that's how she felt, I wasn't gonna pressure her anymore. I figured I needed to let the shit play out. If it was meant to be then it will be. I nodded and walked back to my car.

"Oh, and good morning, G-Baby," I said as looked back at her, and then I hopped in my ride.

She stood in the doorway staring at me. The cami she was sporting had her luscious nipples rock hard, and I couldn't look at her any longer or my dick was gonna get hard.

I started my ignition, and before I pulled off, she hollered out, "Geon!" "Yeah, shorty?"

"Wait… let me grab my shoes." She smirked.

"You must be done ranting and raving? Or you need to curse me out some more to relieve some of that steam," I told her.

"I'm done, and I'm sorry."

"So, what, you riding with a G today?" "Yeah, I'm riding with a G."

"What about yo' clothes?" I chuckled.

"You can buy me some more. You know my size, right?" She smiled, referring to the time I bought her clothes from Walmart.

Aspen ran and got her shoes. She locked up their house

and hopped in my ride.

"Where we going?" "Wherever you wanna go."

"Let's go get a room. I need some rest. I really just want to sleep, not answer any phone calls or nothing," she suggested, and that was even better in my eyes.

"Nice ride, G."

"Nice body, bae," I joked and glanced at her hard nipples. She laughed.

I was digging Aspen like a muthafucka. We checked into the Embassy Suites in downtown Chicago, and they had a spa in the hotel. I wasn't good at this mushy shit, but so far, I was doing my thang with wining and dining my woman. We chilled for two days straight, not once ever having sex. That was something new for me. I was used to digging out bitches' insides then sending them on their way.

Chapter: 15 Asia

Tears fell from my eyes as I looked at the grade Professor Garrett gave me on my midterm paper. I was convinced this nigga had it out for me. I was gonna ask him why the fuck

was that my grade, but instead, I stormed out of class and hopped in my car. I couldn't stop crying. I knew for a fact that this shit was going to hinder me. I needed this class, and I couldn't afford to fail it.

As I drove to the massage parlor, I figured out what I needed to do to get professor Garrett on board with the program. Fuck that, I wasn't going to allow him to embarrass me. I worked too hard throughout this semester to keep being shitted on.

Once I made it to the massage parlor, I walked past Aspen, who was giggling on her phone. She had a smile so broad and wide that I wondered who was making her smile like that.

"What's up, sis?"

"Hey, boo," she spoke back, and I headed toward the back.

I changed into my lil uniform that I wore while I was there, and I tried to take my mind off the bullshit. My phone vibrated in my pocket, and it was Trill. I smiled when I saw his name. We weren't anything exclusive yet, but I was loving me some him.

"Hey." I answered on the first ring. "Whaddup, bae?

Whatchu doing?"

"I'm working right now. What's up with you? How you been, bae?" "I'm good, shorty. Just tryna see you. My mans having a party tonight

for his birthday. It's at a hotel, though. It's a pool party, and I need the baddest bitch in the Chi on my arm in her baddest two piece," he joked, and I laughed.

"Nigga, my thick ass ain't rocking no two-piece swim suit. Shit, this pudge in my stomach gotta go first."

"Man, that ain't shit, just something extra for me to lay my head on after I finish digging out that pussy."

"Boyyyy," I chuckled.

I loved me some Trill. He was always with hell of jokes and a fun ass personality. I hadn't seen him since he'd been back from my New York, and I couldn't wait to wrap my arms around him.

"I'll go. I ain't doing shit else."

"Aight, meet me at my crib at 10:00," he stated. I agreed and hung up the phone.

After work, I was out the door fast as hell. I headed straight to Target to find a bad ass swim suit. I wasn't one of those bitches who thought she had to rock a Gucci or Louie swim suit. Shit, target was just as high, but their swimwear was on point. After finding my swim suit, I went to the nail shop, got a fill-in and a pedicure, and was out the door.

Heading home, I kept yawning. I was low key tired. It was a Friday, and I wanted to crash like a muthafucka.

Instead, I hopped in the shower and pulled myself together. I did my makeup and flat ironed my sew in then I looked at my phone. I had a couple of missed calls from Aruba. I would've answered, but knowing sis, she wanted to go out, and I wanted to spend some time with my man. I missed Trill. Once

I was fully dressed, I walked out my apartment and headed to Trill's condo.

I knocked on his front door, and he opened it, looking at me like I was crazy.

"Man, yo' ass is a nut. It's cold as fuck outside," he said, chuckling at my attire.

I was sporting some short ass shorts and a wife beater with some thigh boots and a red mink fur. It was the middle of October, and the weather was tricky as hell.

"What? I think I look good." I giggled.

"Shidddd, you look beautiful, but it's still cold, and I still don't like them short ass shorts on you, ma. But what's up, baby?" He pulled me close to him, and I stared in his eyes. Our chemistry was everything.

"Hey, bae," I said in a low tone.

I leaned in and slowly kissed his lips.

"I missed yo pretty ass, and I missed her even more." He grabbed my pussy.

"Oh, you grabbing bitches by the pussy now, huh?" I asked him, and he laughed

"Only the ones that belong to me." "Remember, I belong to no one."

"Shit, you gon' always belong to me. But, come on, man, lets go." He grabbed my hand, and we left out the door then hopped in his car.

We talked about everything under the sun. We discussed his recent trip to New York, we discussed his plans to buy property, and I told him about my schooling. It was something when I could be who I really am in front of a man. Trill made me that comfortable.

When we pulled up to the Sybaris, my eyes widened. I

just knew he had something special planned for me. I started smiling like a fool as we got out the car. Trill held my hand as we walked through the lobby and headed toward the suite. I could hear music bumping from down the hall, and I was confused. I guess it really was a party. I felt kind of special because this was the first time that I was meeting any of his friends.

Trill knocked on the door to the party, and it opened. There was hell of weed smoke as we entered, and I started coughing due to all the smoke. He held my hand tight as we went through the crowd. I glanced around, and it was hella bitches; some were topless, some were fully clothed, and some were dressed in bathing suits. The shit was live, but I was skeptical.

"Damn," I whispered as I looked at all the people.

I noticed the room we were in had a connecting room, so the door was open to the other room on the side of it. There were a bunch of people on that side too.

"We got them Young, Rich, Niggas, in the muthafucking building!

Happy Birthday, Menace!" the DJ shouted into the microphone.

"Y'all got a DJ in here? What the hell? How in the hell?" I said, and Trill laughed.

"Yeah, we got the whole fucking floor rented. All these rooms are ours for the night." He grinned, and I nodded.

I was used to dealing with college niggas and not niggas in the streets.

Trill was something totally different for me.

"Aye, bro, this my girl, Asia, and this is my nigga Menace. Today is this nigga's birthday, ma, with his old ass," Trill Joked.

"Happy Birthday!" I held my hand out to shake his hand, but he pulled me in for a hug instead.

"Aye, where G?" he asked.

"He's in the other room where the pool at," he told him and knocked his drink back.

We walked off and went in the room here the pool was. He searched until he found who he was looking for, and as we got closer, my eyes got wider and wider.

"Aspen, what the fuck you doing here?"

I gasped when I saw my sister clad in her bikini, sipping on a margarita, and hugged up on this big, buff ass, tattoo on the face ass nigga. He truly looked like a hoodlum. He had a hoodie on with the hood on his head, he was smoking a blunt, and his arm was draped around Aspen.

"A! Whatchu doing here, bitch?" she scoffed, looking me over.

She had a look of shock written on her face, and I shook my head. She thought she was so slick. I didn't give a fuck about her stepping out on Finesse bitch ass, but it was the point that she was being so damn secretive. Aruba told me about some nigga who came to the job and she left with him.

"I'm here with my friend, but you… who the fuck is this nigga?" I eyed the dude.

"I'm her nigga. Who the fuck is you?"

"I'm her blood, my nigga. I'm her fucking sister," I snapped and rolled my eyes at his ass.

"Aye, ma, calm down. This my nigga, Gangsta. I was actually bringing you over to introduce you to him"

"Hmmm, Aspen, let me holla at you," I stated then grabbed her arm and pulled her away from him.

We went off to a corner of the room, and she glared at me.

"Bitch, you know you ain't my Momma, right?" she stated, and we both laughed because that's what I used to tell her.

"I know, but who is dude? You know I be concerned about you, Aspen."

"You not gonna believe it when I tell you." "Tell me, bitch."

"He's the dude who kidnapped me. Before you say anything, just know that it's just as crazy to me as it is to you. But, we vibe, we have a connection, sis, and it's indescribable," she said with all her teeth showing.

That's how hard she was smiling while talking about this nigga "Wow! All I can fucking say is wow!"

"I know, but please keep that between us. Aruba doesn't know, and I see you just happen to be dating his friend. Girl, it's a small world for real." She giggled, and I knew Aspen was drunk.

"It is, but come on before they get suspicious," I told her.

We walked back over to the guys, and Trill was all smiles. He tried to grab my hand, but I moved it abruptly. Fuck him. He was one of the niggas who robbed us, and I wasn't feeling that shit.

Aspen sat back down next to that nigga, and I rolled my eyes at his ass too then walked off without saying a word to Trill. I was heated. I didn't like to feel like I was being played. In fact, I hated shit like that.

I ordered a Hennessey and coke from the made up ass bar, and I sipped my drink slowly as I pondered what I was going to say to him. He didn't come after me, and that spoke volumes. I wondered if he thought this shit was a game. If he thought I was some type of goofy bitch.

Moments later, as that thought ran across my mind again, Trill came and stood next to me at the make shift bar.

"What's up Lips? You good?" he eyed me, I glanced over at him and rolled my eyes.

"Fuck you, nigga! Hell naw, I ain't good."

"What's with all of that? And don't say that 'Fuck you' shit no more, man, and I'm serious. Don't disrespect me because I don't disrespect you. Now, again, what's good?

"I just don't deal with liars. You robbed the massage parlor with your friends, and you knew where my sister was the entire time. You could've told me the truth when you saw how worried I was about her. You ain't shit," I snapped at him.

"True, I knew where your sister was the entire time, but it wasn't my place to disclose that info. Secondly, Gangsta is my homie, and my loyalty lied with him. That's why I told you not to be worried because I knew she was in good hands, and more importantly, I didn't know you had anything to do with that massage parlor. It was just a coincidence when I saw you. I didn't mean for that shit to go down," he explained, and I just looked at him.

"I don't like liars, Trill. If anything, you should've come clean with me,"

"I don't lie, Lips, and you fucking know it. So, stop acting like this shit was a whole deception type of thing. Shit happens; it was just a coincidence. Muthafuckas fall for each other, and then again, shit happens. I understand you're pissed, but honestly, don't hold that shit against me. That ain't cool, ma."

"You think I shouldn't hold that against you? Come on now. We all have skeletons, but I thought we were better than that. Shit, we been keeping it real with each another since we met, but I guess that's a lie too. You know what? I'm not even comfortable here anymore. I'm gonna take an Uber and go the fuck home." I stormed away from him and out of the hotel room.

"Aye, man, where the fuck you going?" he barked, pulling my arm.

I snatched away from him. "Trill, let me go," I snapped.

We were in the hallway, and even though the music was blasting, I knew somebody heard my loud ass mouth. He stared at me intensely, and I knew he felt the negative energy that I was shooting his way. He had me fucked up.

"Man, bring yo ass on," he growled.

Trill grabbed me by my elbow and held it tight.

I tried to pull away, but his strength was unmatched. He was hurting my fucking elbow as he dragged me to a room down the hall from the party. He used the digital key thing on his phone to open the room door, and we both entered in the room.

Looking around, I gasped at what I saw. The room was decked out with pink roses petals on the bed and on the floor. There was a bottle of Moet sitting in an ice bucket and some chocolate covered strawberries on a platter on the table.

"Who fucking room is this?" I asked, trying to hold my smile in.

"It was for us for after the party, but since yo ass tripping right now, I needed to bring you in this bitch to talk some sense into yo ass," he spat.

I could tell he was pissed at me.

"Well, I don't wanna hear shit you got to say." I crossed my arms over my chest, trying to play off how I really felt. I had forgiven him already, and he didn't even know it.

"Man, look, if you wanna fuck with me, it's some things you gotta get understood. I'm a street, nigga, and I do street nigga shit. I make my bread in the streets. Love me now or love me when I'm gone because the way I live my life, Imma be gone one day soon, ma, and that's just some real ass spill for you. The system might take me, or I might be dead. But instead of bitching at me, learn how to deal with what comes with it. Instead of getting mad, learn how to talk and stop running away. We ain't gon' make it if you keep doing goofball ass shit like that."

"Don't say that shit about being dead," I scoffed, ignoring everything else he said.

"I'm just saying. Now stop being mean to me and come here," he urged then flopped on the bed and gave me those sexy ass bedroom eyes.

He bit his bottom lip, and I could've creamed on myself right then and there. This man was sexy as fuck.

"Fuck you, nigga." I rolled my eyes, trying to play hard to get. "Did you just hear what I said, man?"

"Whatever, Trill."

"I said, come here, Lips," he demanded, and I walked over to him.

I stood between his legs and looked down at him while he looked up a me.

"Lips, I ain't a perfect nigga, but I'm a real one. I apologize about not coming clean with you, but rock with nigga. I promise I'm gon' make this shit worth it," he said, and I smiled.

"I'm rocking, but I swear you better not lie to me anymore, Trill. No more secrets, or I'm gonna be done with yo ass for real." I leaned down and kissed his lips, and he pulled me on top of him.

"You ain't goin' no muthafucking where, so kill all that noise. No come ride daddy's dick. I wanna see them titties bounce." He grinned, and I happily agreed.

Me and Trill fucked for the remainder of the night. We never went back to the party, and that was fine with me. I was laid up with my boo and enjoying it.

MONDAY MORNING ROLLED AROUND, and I had my

game face on. I was at the massage parlor earlier than anyone. It wasn't even open yet, and I was sitting out here. My whole plan was to get Professor Garrett to see things my way. I sat patiently in my car smoking a blunt and looking at the few pictures in my phone that I took of Trill's sleeping silhouette. I don't know what made me take those pictures of him, but he looked so peaceful and sexy as hell sleeping.

I spotted Aspen's car and saw that she was in the car with Finesse. I didn't know what the fuck she was doing. I swear that nigga Gangsta looked crazy as fuck. I wouldn't dare play those type of games with his ass. I watched as she leaned in and kissed Finesse on the lips. This bitch was trying it.

She hopped out the car, and Finesse got in the driver's seat. I put out my blunt and got out my car. She looked over and noticed me.

"Bitch, whatchu doing here so early? And on a Monday on top of that?" she asked.

"Girl, I told you I needed this extra day. I need to make this money," I told her.

"Oh, well, yeah, we need the extra help anyway since Dyna quit, and Ru started working at the county." She smiled and opened the door.

We entered the massage parlor and turned on the lights. It was time for us to get our day started.

"Aspen, answer me this... What the hell are you doing playing with that big ass nigga and Finesse? Hunty, you look like you want some problems fucking with them two niggas."

"I got this, believe me." She exhaled, and I guess she didn't wanna go into details about it.

Time seemed to move slowly as I waited for Professor Garrett. I picked up all of Dyna's clients, and I didn't understand how these bitches did this shit. Seeing a dick wasn't something new to me, but seeing multiple dicks in one setting was. I massaged the men, and when they flipped over, I gave them a hand job to complete the job. Afterward, I was paid. Some bitches were fucking in those rooms, but I wish a muthafucka would ask me to fuck.

Seconds later, a knock on the room door startled me from my thoughts. I changed my voice. "One second."

I could hear Garrett talking to Aspen, and a smile came across my face. I placed a face mask on and put on the blonde bob wig that I had purchased yesterday from the beauty supply store.

I opened the door, and professor Garrett walked in and eyed me. I glanced down, so he wouldn't notice my eyes.

"Hello, you're new," he spoke, and I only nodded.

He got undressed and then wrapped the towel around his waist and lay on his stomach on the table.

"Would you like your oil warm or not?" I asked.

"I would like the eucalyptus, and of course I would like it warm," he said.

I got the oil he requested and warmed it. While he was waiting, I took my phone out and propped it up on the counter. I started recording.

I gave him a great back massage along with his legs, and calves and his buttocks. By the time he flipped over, he was so relaxed that he still hadn't opened his eyes. I was so busy focusing on my job that I almost forgot about my plan. I snatched the wig off my head, when it was time for me to beat his dick off. I looked into the camera and smiled as I slowly stroked his dick. He moaned lightly, and I held back my laugh. He sounded like a bitch.

It took him all of five minutes to cum, and I was ecstatic.

"Young lady, that was awesome." He was breathing hard, and his eyes were still closed.

"Thanks, Professor Garrett," I spoke, and his eyes shot open. "What the hell!" he barked out, staring at me with wide eyes. hurriedly, I grabbed my phone and shut off the camera. "Asia Walters?" he said as if he couldn't believe it. "The one and fucking only, Professor."

"What… I… I… didn't know. I would never engage in anything with a student," he tried to explain.

"Ummm, yeah, okay. But I got you on video, professor. And if you don't want me to show it to the world, I need you to change my fucking grades. I cannot afford to retake your class." I scoffed.

"You're blackmailing me?"

"You call it that, I call it both of us getting what we want. And, believe it or not, it doesn't matter that I'm your student. This is illegal anyway. This is a form of prostitution, and technically, Professor Garrett, you're a john. Please don't make me embarrass you. Please hear me when I say I need my grades changed." I smirked and walked out of the massage room, leaving him to his thoughts.

If professor Garrett knew like I knew, he would do as I said or face the consequences.

Chapter:16 Trill

"Baeeeeeeee, come on, I'm fucking hungry!" Lips squealed as I checked underneath the hood of my car.

She was hungry, and I was too, but I needed to make

sure my ride was straight.

"Here I come. We gon' take the Benz." I scoffed looking at my truck.

My truck was my baby, the first ride I bought when I had a couple thousand in my pockets, and now it was fucking all the way up. Asia walked into my crib to grab her purse, and as I put the hood down on my truck, my cell vibrated in my pocket. Pulling it out, I saw that Nika was calling me.

I ain't talked to this bitch since before I went to New York. I smashed her only because Asia liked to play games, and she was some quick and easy pussy to catch a nut from before I took flight. As soon as I was about to answer her phone call, Asia walked outside, and I didn't wanna be rude and disrespectful by hopping on the phone.

"I'm ready, bae."

We hopped in my Benz and headed to Ruth's Chris steak house. I had already made reservations.

As we sat down to eat, my phone wouldn't stop vibrating. Asia kept glancing up at me as she looked over the menu, and I looked around.

If you don't answer that damn phone, Rahmeek," she stated, calling me by my government, and I laughed.

"Awww shit, what I do? I gotchu calling me Rahmeek."

"You ain't do shit. I'm just sayin' why you not answering that vibrating ass phone?"

"Because I'm with you, and my phone isn't important right now.

That's why. Anything else?" I questioned, and she smirked.

"Nope, I'm good."

The waitress came and took our orders, and then we engaged in small talk.

"Me and the homies got a job to do real soon, but afterward, I wanna take you out the country. I feel like we both need a change of scenery," I told her, and she smiled.

"Yes, I'm with it. Between school and work, I need a fucking break, ya know?"

"Hell yeah, shit is getting real. What plans does yo family have for thanksgiving and shit?"

"I don't know yet. Me and my sisters are close with our parents, but not that close. We don't hear about shit until maybe three of four days before the event." She shrugged it off, and the waitress brought over our drinks.

As we continued to talk, a group of maybe ten to fifteen women came in the restaurant. I guess they were celebrating someone's birthday, but I noticed them because they were loud as fuck.

As they sat down, I spotted Nika in the crowd. She spotted me as well. When I saw her march toward me, I cursed under my breath. I knew it was about to be some shit. She couldn't help herself. She was always with the fucking drama. It's crazy what a nigga had to go through.

"You ain't hear your phone?" she said, standing in front of me.

I picked my drink up and sipped it, not bothering to even respond. I wasn't with that drama shit, and I hated to be embarrassed in public.

"You don't hear me fucking talking to you, Trill?" she snapped, and I looked up at her goofy ass.

"I hear you, but don't you see me eating right now? Fuck is up with you?"

"See, nigga, you like to play too many fucking games. You talked when you was fucking me just two weeks ago, and now you sitting here with this bitch acting like you don't know who the fuck I am. Stop playing with me, nigga, before I go clean in on you and this bitch," Nika threatened.

Asia placed her drink down. She held a smirk on her face, and I knew some shit was about to pop off.

"Bitch, who the fuck you think you playing with?" Asia spoke in a low tone.

"Girl, hush, this ain't got shit to do with you. I'm talking to this lame ass nigga right here."

"Bitch, if you don't move the fuck away from this table, I'm gon' drag yo ass, hoe," Asia threatened.

She was still speaking in a low tone, only loud enough for us to hear her. I guess she didn't like being embarrassed in public either. I understood completely.

"Fuck you, bitch. You ain't dragging shit but yo' dumb ass to the welfare office. Just like me when this lame ass nigga gets you popped off and forgets you even fucking exist. Don't think you got a winner, bitch, 'cause he's far from that," Nika expressed, and my eyes widened.

The fuck was she talking about?

"Bitch, chill, you doing too much. These niggas for everybody, hunty.

I'm far from pressed." Asia finally spoke, and I glared at her.

I didn't want her to feed into Nika's bullshit.

"Bitch, getcho dumb ass the fuck away from me making a scene," I said.

"Fuck you, Trill. You gonna learn one day about playing with women's hearts." She scoffed and then she went in her purse.

The first thing I thought was this bitch was about to pull out a gun, but she pulled out a pregnancy test and dropped that bitch in the glass that held my drink.

"Congratulations, Papa."

She smirked. Asia got up and walked out the restaurant while Nika stood there grinning like shit was all good. I was fucking heated. If this bitch was pregnant, it was a strong possibility that it wasn't mine. This hoe was fucking everybody in the hood, and it was my fault that I gave the bitch some of my fucking time. I regretted that shit like a muthafucka right now.

"Bitch, I know you ain't just drop yo piss in my muthafucking drink," I spewed angrily.

She thought shit was funny, but I had a trick for her ditzy ass.

"Hell, yeah, I did. I'm tired of you trying to play me, nigga!" Nika snapped.

I grabbed her elbow and tightened my grip on it.

"Walk the fuck away, Nika. You want to put on a show, and if I give you what you looking for, you ain't gon' like it," I spat in a low tone.

She stormed off, and I stood up and went outside to look for Asia. Just that fast, she was fucking gone.

"PLEASEEEE... Pleaseeee, Trill! Don't make me do this!" Nika cried as I we sat in front of Planned Parenthood. This bitch had me fucked up if she thought she wasn't about to have an abortion.

"Nah, bitch, you wanted to show yo ass, right? Getcho dumb ass out the car so we can take care of ya lil problem. I'm gonna make sure you don't have your dumb ass in the welfare line because it won't be my seed in yo ass."

A week had passed since that shit happened between me and Nika, and Asia hadn't once called me back or returned my text messages. She hasn't even been to school, or either she was taking a different route to fucking avoid me. I missed her lil ass like crazy, and I knew Nika having this baby was gonna fuck everything up for us.

"I swear I won't bother you, Trill, I swear I won't. If you don't wanna be a part of the baby's life, I'll leave you alone, but please don't make me abort my baby," she cried.

Her tears fell rapidly from her eyes, and I didn't care. This was her doing. She brought this shit upon herself. She should've known fucking better than to be fucking with a nigga like me.

"Nah, yo ass wanted to put on a show, right? You wanted my attention, right? Well, I'm giving it to you right now. Get the fuck out the car before I drag yo ass out, Nika, and that's on my momma."

"Trill."

"Nah, ain't no, Trill. Listen, you brought that ratchet, ghetto shit to me while I was out eating dinner, and you thought it was cool to show yo ass that night. You know I hate that loud shit, but you tried it any fucking way. Now, look at ya dumb ass. I don't feel no fucking sympathy for you. Imma tell you now, get the fuck outta the car, Nika."

"Trill... Trill, please," she cried, but I wasn't hearing that shit, and her saying my name only irritated me more.

"Bitch, say my name one more time, and I'm gonna fuck you up!" I growled.

I wasn't gonna put my hands on her; I just wanted to scare her ass into doing what the fuck I said. She slowly eased out the car, and I followed. She had me fucked up. I didn't know what the fuck she thought this shit was, but it wasn't a game at all. She entered the clinic and gave them her name. They escorted her to the back, and I sat there patiently.

A couple hours later, I dropped her off at home. She wept silently in the front seat, and I low key felt bad, but not that fucking bad. She tried it. When I pulled up to her crib, she hopped out my ride and slammed the door as hard as she could.

"I'ma talk to you lata, aight?" I hollered, and she stuck her middle finger up at me.

I definitely didn't give a fuck that she was in her feelings. I was trying to build something with Asia, and she fucked that up showing her ass.

I headed toward my mom's crib because I hadn't seen my lil brother in a while. When I pulled up, I spotted Asia's car, and a smile grew on my face. I was happy that she was there. Maybe she would talk to me.

Once I got out my car, I hurriedly went inside. I spotted my mother in the kitchen, and I gave her a hug and a kiss. I then headed into the den where I knew Asia and Rico would be.

They both had their heads in the books. She was sitting a lil too close to him for my liking.

"What's good, y'all?' I asked them, making them both look up. "Whaddup, big bro." I dapped Rico up, but Asia just looked at me and

turned her head back to the book.

"You ain't' speaking to a nigga, Lips?" I eyed her, and she

was still silent.

"Rico, I'll call you later," she said and closed her book.

Asia grabbed her bag and headed for the door, walking right past me like she didn't know who I was.

I was right behind her as she flew out the door. She powered walked fast as hell to her car, but I grabbed her elbow and turned her around to face me.

"So, that's it, Ma? You gonna keep curving a nigga? I'm trying to talk to you. What's up?"

"What do we got to talk about, Trill? I just explained to you that I didn't like liars, and yet you lied to me. You were fucking with that girl way harder than you led me to believe. And she's pregnant," she snapped, and it seemed like tears formed in her eyes.

I didn't wanna see her cry.

"Man, look, that shit was a misunderstanding. You gotta believe me. Yeah, I was fucking with her, but it wasn't that deep. Bitches be lying, Lips, and you know that shit. Plus, she ain't pregnant no more."

"Well, good. I wasn't tryna play step mommy, but you know what, I've been doing a lot of thinking lately, and this is becoming too much for me. It was fun while it lasted, but thinking about my education right now is much more important than some hood rat ass drama," she snapped and stormed away toward her car.

"So, whatchu saying?"

"I'm saying were through, Trill. I'm saying have a nice life with you and your baby momma." She hopped in her ride and peeled away after that.

I stood in front of my mom's crib feeling like a dumb ass. Nika had just fucked up the potential relationship me and Asia were trying to build. Nah, better yet, I just fucked that up.

Chapter: 17 Aspen

Cleaning the house, I had my stereo on blast. Throwback 2 Chainz was blaring through the speakers, and I had the house smelling like good ole lemon Pine Sol. I was in a good fucking mood

today. I had spent an entire week with Gangsta, and Finesse didn't question my whereabouts but only one time. I told him I took a trip with Aruba, and he went for that shit.

Gangsta was someone special to me. I didn't know what it was, but me and him were everything when we were together. He was rough, but he was gentle, and I was falling for him more and more every day. The crazy shit is, I couldn't walk away from Finesse, and I didn't understand why. What was holding me back? I think it was the fact that I liked cheating on Finesse because he cheated on me so many times. It felt good to know I was getting him back. The shit sounded crazy, but it was the truth.

The doorbell rang, and I turned down the music, so I could answer it. I ordered some shoes, and I assumed that it was those that were coming. I swung the door open, and my mouth dropped when I saw who was standing on the other side. My instincts told me to beat her ass, but I knew I wouldn't be able to. I was already pissed when I learned she was in my house while I was kidnapped.

"Kari, why the fuck are you at my house?" I growled, eyeing her up and down.

"I need to speak with Finesse."

Her face was frowned up, and I chuckled.

"You're looking for him now, huh? Well, he ain't here. Nigga ain't been here in two days. So, I don't know what to tell you." I shrugged, lying my ass off.

He had been there because he wanted to spend time with me since I've been back home.

"Tell him when you do see him, that his son needs some clothes and shoes," she spat, and my eyes widened.

I looked at the little boy who was with her, and he looked like Finesse. He was way older, though. This little boy was like six years old at least. It couldn't be his son.

"Bitch, leave my fucking house before I beat your ass in front of your son," I scolded her.

I didn't know what else to say. I wanted to go the fuck off, but I didn't wanna go extreme in front of the little boy. But my heart just broke as I looked at him. I knew deep down inside that he was Finesse's son.

She turned around and grabbed the little boy's hands. They walked off to her red Benz and peeled off. My heart started to race, and I couldn't believe my ears. As a matter of fact, I couldn't believe my eyes. He was messing with Kari wayyyy before me. He had to have been. Oh my god. Tears fell from my eyes as I thought about Finesse having a kid.

I've been through some much with him, and you know what? This was fucking it! I called Finesse's phone, and he didn't answer, so I left him a message telling him to come home ASAP. I didn't even finish cleaning; I went up the stairs to my bedroom and lay down. This shit wasn't life right now.

MY MIND WAS all over the place. My bags were packed, but my heart was torn, I had to move outta this crib with Finesse. I loved him, but I wasn't in love with him. Finesse never came home last night. He never called back. He really doesn't give a fuck, and I know it. As of today, I was officially done.

I was going to move in with Aruba until I found a place. My mind was scrambled, and I all I really wanted right now was a clearer head. Keys jingled in the door, and I looked up. Seeing Finesse come through the door made me second guess my decision. I was expecting to be gone before he even came in the house.

He walked inside and eyed me. I looked away because I felt guilty. I was just gonna leave without even telling him. I had to do it that way. I knew I wouldn't be able to walk out the door while he was there. I didn't have the strength.

"So, what's this? Whatchu doing?"

"I'm leaving, Finesse," I said in a low tone.

"This how you gonna do that shit? You gonna walk out the door without even telling a nigga first, huh?"

"I'm telling you now."

"Why you Leaving, Aspen? You fucking with someone else now?" he questioned, trying to play reverse psychology.

I shook my head. I was lying, but I didn't have the heart to tell him that there was someone else. As much shit as he put me through, I still cared about his feelings. I shouldn't even care about his feelings seeing as how he has a son out here in the fucking world.

"Aight, bitch, do whatever the fuck you wanna do. Get the fuck outta my crib, and don't look back this muthafucking way," he snapped, and my eyes widened.

He was like Dr. Jekyll and Mr. Hyde. What the fuck?

"See, that's the muthafucking problem right there, Finesse! Look at you! Look at how you fucking talk to me! I'm sick of this shit! I'm sick of being sick and fucking tired! I've gave you all of me! At twenty-five years old, I feel like I'm fifty because I've been dealing with a man who doesn't love me."

"I do love you, Aspen, and you know it! You probably let them ratchet ass sisters of yours put that shit in your fucking head. Ole dumb ass," he shot back, and I laughed.

"No, Finesse! Don't nobody gotta tell me that I should leave you. You don't think my sisters know how you treat me. You don't think my sisters told me you had a bitch in this house and my dumb ass never said shit to you about it? So, yeah, I'm real fucking dumb when it comes to this bullshit. And fuck you, finesse!"

"Aspen, if I didn't love you, I wouldn't have taken care of you all these years, If I didn't love you, I wouldn't put you first. You talking some greasy ass shit right now, and you faulting a nigga for making a mistake."

I chuckled when he said that shit.

"The same fucking mistake you've been making for years! Get the fuck outta here with that shit! You don't love me. You love the thought of me! You love the thought of a bitch sitting in your big ass house, because this was never my house to begin with, while you run the streets doing whatever the fuck you want with whoever the fuck you want! But, me, you don't fucking love me! If you loved me, you would have never fucking cheated on me! If you loved me, you would've brought your ass home time and time again, but you fucking didn't!" I shouted as tears fell from my face. I was hurting so bad from all the shit I had endured over the years from him.

"You knew what and who I was when you fucking met me! I'm the nigga who put them jewels around your neck, I'm the nigga who bought you a fucking Benz truck. I did that shit! You a fucking church girl. Bitch, yo' ass wouldn't have shit if it wasn't for me," he snapped, and I just looked at him.

"And you wouldn't have shit either if it wasn't for me! Please, let's not forget. It was your money, but it was my smarts that got you ahead in life. You should be thanking me, you bastard!" I shot back.

I taught him the art of making something out of nothing. He knew nothing firsthand about getting a business. I taught his ass how to get life insurance policies and to pay on them so his momma or me if I ever became his wife had something tucked away in case the streets ever claimed his ass. He knew nothing about having a back account and savings account. This church girl taught his ass a lot of shit.

"Leave, if you gonna leave then, Aspen. I'm not holding you back at all," he said in a calm voice.

He didn't have to say anything else. Me and Finesse's time has expired.

I grabbed my suitcases and headed for the door. He sat on his couch looking off into space like he didn't give a fuck.

"Oh, and by the way, I met you son by Kari yesterday as well. You have some good genes, he's very handsome," I spat and headed out the door.

I put my bags in the trunk of my car and started my ignition. I cried the entire time I drove after I called Aruba and told her I was on my way.

My cell rang, and it was Gangsta calling me. I hadn't heard from him since I'd been back. I answered the phone on the second ring.

"Hey." I wiped my tears with the back of my hand. "Fuck you crying for?" he barked into the phone. "It's nothing. I'm fine." I sniffled.

"Come on, G-Baby. Don't tell me anything. Where you at?"

"I'm leaving Finesse's crib, and I'm on my way to my sister's house.

What's up?"

"Come to my house right now. I need to see ya face," he spoke and hung up the phone.

Gangsta was rude as fuck like that. I made a detour and headed for Gangsta's house. I wanted him to wrap his big, massive arms around me and just hold me.

When I made it to his house, I got out the car and rang the doorbell. He instantly opened the door like he was standing on the other side and waiting for me.

"What's good my baby?"

I wrapped my arms around his neck and broke down crying. He picked me up bridal style and carried me up the stairs to his bedroom. After laying me in his bed, he lay in front of me, and I buried my face in his chest.

"Whatever it is, I'm right here. Don't worry about shit ever again. I got chu forever, ma, and that's on everything I love," he whispered and kissed the top of my head.

At that moment, I knew he was the man for me. No man has ever told me that we had forever. And all I ever wanted was that forever thing with someone.

Chapter: 18 Asia

Looking at my final grade, I was pissed. Professor Garrett had me fucked up. He was calling my bluff about this video. He must've thought I wasn't gonna do it, well he had another thing coming.

Once my final class let out, I raced to the library and logged on to the school newspaper. I uploaded the video in the comments section and the pictures as well. He was going to regret the day he fucked with me.

Afterward, I left the library and headed to my next class. I wasn't going to be the only muthafucka around here pissed off.

I didn't think he understood how him failing me would affect my GPA. I worked my ass off, and it still didn't seem good enough for him.

My phone vibrated as I walked to my next class. Pulling it out of my purse, I looked at it and saw that it was Trill texting me. He had been texting me since I walked out the restaurant on his ass. I was sick with disgust when that bitch came and acted a fool on our ass.

I didn't do the drama shit well. I'll beat a bitch up, but I wasn't ratchet in the streets. That's not my M.O. I couldn't lie if I wanted to; I missed Trill crazy ass like a muthafucka. It's been killing me to give him the silent treatment.

T: I miss you, Lips

After reading the text message, I caved and called him. I missed him too.

"Hey bae," he answered "Hey, Rahmeek."

He chuckled hearing me say his first name. "That always means we into it."

"We not into it, why you say that?" I laughed.

"The only time you call me Rahmeek is when you mad at a nigga"

"I am mad at you." I smiled as I spoke into the phone.

The phone was pressed tightly against my ear when a ding sound came through. I looked at the phone, and it was an email notification. I put Trill on speaker and opened the email. Just like I knew it would, the video of Professor Garrett that I uploaded was circulating. A smirk came upon my face because I knew it would happen.

"So, whatchu say, ma? You down?" Trill's voice broke my train of thought.

"Oh, huh?"

"I said can I come over tonight? I think we need to talk." "Yeah, you can come over."

"You miss me, huh? And don't lie, Asia, I know you do. We vibe too heavy for you not to miss me."

"Yeah, I miss you," I admitted as I made it to the door of Professor Garrett's class.

"Aight, I'll see you when you get out of school. Call me as soon as you leave."

"Okay, I will." I hung up the phone and entered the class-room.

As soon as I did, I noticed everyone looking in their phone whispering and laughing. The shit had gone viral right away. I didn't give a fuck as I smiled happily all the ways to my seat. Professor Garrett even looked down at his phone. He cleared his throat and began to speak, but I could see his bald head drenched with sweat, and it wasn't even hot in the class.

I told him not to fuck with me, and he did anyway. now this was the price he had to pay.

I listened to his lecture and looked at the time on my phone. His class was an hour and a half, and I was bored already.

As the class progressed. There was a knock on the classroom door. The door opened, and in walked the provost.

"Professor Garrett, I need to speak with you for a moment," he said to him.

Me and the professor locked eyes, and he stepped out of the class. Everyone started whispering about the video, cracking jokes, and much more. It took Professor Garrett about fifteen minutes to come back in the classroom, and his red skin looked flushed.

He finished his lecture and dismissed the class. As I was about to walk out, he stopped me.

"Asia, may I speak with you?"

"What's up?" I acted perfectly normal, even though I knew what it was. He walked over and closed the classroom door.

"Do you know what you have done?" He glared at me. "No, do you know what you have done?" I shot back.

"I cannot give you a grade that you don't deserve! It's unethical, and I refuse to be blackmailed into doing so."

"You being at a massage parlor is unethical, with yo' married ass," I snapped, and he shook his head.

He started pacing the floor, and he seemed off to me. It felt like he was about to do something to me. He walked closer to me and stood in my face. He was so close that he could kiss me.

"I've worked my ass off for thirty got damn years, and just like that, it's going down the drain because of that video! Do you know what the fuck you've done to me, huh?" he shouted, and his spittle flew in my face.

I took two steps back.

"Professor Garrett, we had this conversation already. I told you what the consequences were gonna be if you gave me another bad grade, and you called my bluff. Well, I had to show you that I'm not bullshitting. I don't have the money to retake this class if I fail. What part of that don't you understand?"

"Call your bluff? Do you think my life is a joke? Do you think my career is a game? What kind of trivial bullshit is this? I just lost my job today! I've embarrassed my wife and my daughter. And you think it's all fun and games." H raced over to his desk and fumbled inside.

I moved as fast as I could to the door.

"Stop right fucking there," he shouted at me as soon as I got my hand on the door knob.

I turned around and was faced the barrel of a gun. He was a teacher.

Why did he even have a gun on campus?

I dropped my books that I was holding and held my hands up. "Professor, I'm sorry... but you don't have to do this," I stuttered as

reality set in that I just may have fucked up.

At this point, he had tears steaming down his face.

"It's the holidays. I have a family to feed. My reputation is on the line. Thirty years of hard work all down the drain because of a fucking video. Me and my wife were already struggling, and you go and do this... Why would you do this?" his voice cracked, and I instantly felt bad.

I may have gone too fucking far, and now I was about to

pay for it. "I'm… I'm sorry," I apologized again, but I didn't think he got it. "You're not sorry, you bitch! All of this could've been avoided if you

would have just been doing your fucking work! Accept the grade given to you and move the fuck on!" he yelled, and he looked like a mad man.

He started pacing again, this time tapping the gun against his temple then aiming it at me. At this point, I was scared shit less and scared to move.

"I'm not gonna be able to face my wife. I can't," he sobbed, and I felt sorry for him.

Professor Garrett stopped pacing and eyed me. Then, cocked the gun, and my heart raced. He aimed in my direction, and I swallowed hard. It was all over for me.

"I'm sorry too," he said as tears fell from his eyes.

I closed my eyes, and when the gun went off, I was wasn't hit. I opened my eyes, and Professor Garrett's brains were splattered against the chalkboard.

"Oh my Goddddd… No, Mr. Garrettttttttttt," I cried and ran over to him.

I bent down and picked the gun up but then dropped it back to the floor. His eyes were open, but there were no signs of life in them.

"Ooohhhh, no, no, no."

I had to go get someone. I raced out of the class and found campus security, who I escorted back into the classroom. My head was officially messed up after seeing my teacher blow his fucking brains out.

I COULDN'T STOP CRYING as I pulled up to my house. I never called Trill because I had been at the school for four hours. Kids were crying, and so was some of the staff. Everyone kept asking me how I was doing since it was said that I was the last one in the class with him. Honestly, I was mentally fucked up. I drove him to commit suicide because I was being spiteful.

As soon as I got out my car, Trill was standing in front of my building.

I threw my arms around him and sobbed.

"What's up, Lips? What's wrong?" he asked with concern lacing his voice.

"I... I didn't mean it. I swear I didn't," I sobbed.

My hands were shaking as I pulled away from him and tried to open the downstairs door. Trill took the keys from my hand and opened the door himself. We went inside and headed to my apartment. Once inside, he ran me a bath, and I told him all that went down.

"Stop crying, Lips. It's not your fault, ma." His voice was soothing as he washed my back

"But it is."

"Nah, it ain't. You can't blame yo' self for that shit. He committed suicide because that was something he's been planning to do anyway. It was too easy for him to do it. People be having real life issues, ma, and you can't tell what demons are eating a person up"

"Thank You." I looked at him and smiled. "Thank me for what?"

"For being here right now."

"I'm supposed to be by your side always. Don't thank me for shit I'm supposed to do as your nigga, ma. You good, I promise you." I gently kissed his lips, and he sat with me in the bathroom until I was ready to get out.

Three days had passed, and Professor Garrett's suicide had been all over the news. Some were calling it a murder since I ran away from the scene, but that was far from the truth. Every time the news aired it, Trill would change the channel.

In the three days that I've been in the house, Trill stuck to his word haven't left my side. We hadn't even had sex, and that was surprising for both of us. He cooked for me, helped me shower, and held me at night when I had nightmares.

I finally felt a little better today, and I decided to cook him breakfast this morning. Trill was still sleeping, and I was in the kitchen whipping some shit up. My cell chimed, and it was Aruba calling me.

"Hey sis," I answered on the first ring. "Hey, heffa, where're you at?" she asked. "I'm at home. What's up?" I questioned.

"Have you heard from Aspen? She was supposed to come to my house after she left Finesse, but she never made it"

"No, I haven't talked to her in about a week. Don't get too worried just yet. Knowing Aspen, she's still with Finesse."

"Yeah, you're right. But how you doing? I saw a professor at your school killed himself."

I swallowed hard when she said that.

"Yeah, that shit is crazy, but I'm good. Sis, let me call you back," I said and immediately hung up without waiting for her reply.

Once my breakfast was done, I went in my bedroom where Trill was sprawled out sleeping. I threw the cover off him and climbed on the bed. He only had on his boxers, and he was looking so good. I pulled his dick from his boxers and inserted him in my mouth. I slowly sucked the head of his dick, causing him to groan.

"Damn, Lipssssss," he hissed, finally waking up. He looked down at me while I looked up at him.

I had missed his dick just as much as I missed him.

I sucked his ass dry, and then he was finally up. I brought him his breakfast in bed and climbed in with him. We watched television while he chomped down on his food.

"Damn, this shit good as fuck, bae," he said with a full mouth. "Thanks, but close ya damn mouth, nigga," I laughed.

There was a knock on my apartment door. "Who the fuck is that?"

Trill frowned, and I shrugged. I didn't have a clue. I got out of bed to answer the door, and Trill was right behind me.

I looked through the peephole, and I was confused as fuck when I spotted who It was. The fuck?

"It's the police," I whispered to Trill.

"The police? The fuck they want?" he questioned as he moved me to the side then opened the door.

'How can I help y'all?" he asked.

"We have an arrest warrant for Ms. Asia Walters," the detective said, and my eyes widened.

I stepped in front Trill. "For what?" I screeched.

"For the murder of Jason Garrett," he said and stepped stepping into my apartment then turned me around. He placed the cold steel on my wrists, and I broke down in tears.

"Y'all have it all wrong! I didn't do nothing," I sobbed as they led me out of my crib.

"Asia, don't say shit. Don't say shit, bae! I'm calling my lawyer right now, ma," Trill shouted, but I was heartbroken that I was going to jail.

It seemed like my life was crumbling around me, and fast.

Chapter: 19 Gangsta

Looking at Aspen's pretty ass face as she lay asleep, my thoughts started to roam. I was feeling her heavy, and I was happy she walked away from that bitch ass nigga Finesse. We could start

building something great. If it was up to me, she would've been walked away from the fuck nigga. I didn't like to see her hurting.

I haven't felt this way about a woman in a long fucking time. I always wanted to see her with a smile on her face. If I could make that happen for her, I was willing to do anything possible.

When my job was to kill her, I knew without a doubt that I would do it, but once I got to know her, I knew that it was gonna be impossible to go through with it. I just didn't understand how you can love someone you never had a sexual connection with. Believe me, I wanted to tear her ass up, fuck the shit out of her, but I also didn't want her to feel like all I wanted her for was sex.

"You're up early," Aspen's voice boomed from behind me.

I turned around and looked at her. A smile eased on my face.

"I'm an early riser, baby. What's up? How you feeling this morning?" I asked.

"I'm good, especially since I'm here with you."

She smiled and eased out of the bed then kissed me on the cheek as she walked past and headed for the bathroom. I could hear her use the washroom then turn the water on before I could hear her brushing her teeth. Next, the shower was running. I loved a clean woman. Since we'd been kicking it, I noticed her hygiene. She didn't play that lazy shit, and that was attractive as fuck to me.

Aspen waltzed out the bathroom with her long braids dangling in her face. She was about to walk past me, but I grabbed her by her waist and sat her down on my lap.

"You okay?" she asked. "I'm good. You okay?" "Yessss." She giggled.

"Man, this shit feels weird as hell to me right now. You know that, right?"

"And why is that?" she asked.

"Because, I haven't been with a woman like this in a long fucking time."

"Well, I'm happy I'm that woman. I haven't felt this special in a long time." She grinned.

"Kiss me, shawty," I commanded.

She leaned down and kissed me, and I slid my tongue in her mouth.

Grabbing her by the back of her head, our kiss became intense.

The sound of someone kicking in my door caused me to throw Aspen off my lap and onto the floor.

"Get underneath the bed and hide now," I growled as I grabbed my twin Glocks from between my mattress.

I headed out of my bedroom and came face to face with Kozlov, his men, Finesse, and Lanay. Confusion filled my face as

I aimed my twin Glocks. I would die before I let any harm come to Aspen.

"Y'all niggas got one chance, and one chance only to explain why the fuck you just kicked in my door," I questioned no one in particular.

"My Young Gangsta, why didn't you complete the job?" Kozlov asked me with a cigar hanging from his mouth.

"I couldn't do it. I told y'all niggas that."

"And yet, after we had the meeting, you agreed that you would. Now that I hear you're playing house with her, things have gotten out of hand. You're fucking with my money, Gangsta, and I do not approve," Kozlov growled, and I smirked.

"I paid you, nigga. You either gon' kill this bitch or give me my bread back," Finesse chimed in, and I glared at him.

"Nigga, fuck you! I took yo' shit like you took my shit!" I barked. "That's not what we agreed on when we had the meeting. You agreed

to squash the beef. It's been years, Geon," Finesse shot back.

See, let me take y'all back to the meeting that I had with Kozlov when I let Aspen go.

Walking in Kozlov's loft in Miami, my emotions ran high. I knew I had fucked up when I let Aspen go. My heart was pulling me in a different direction than my head. I was supposed to kill her, and I couldn't bring myself to do it.

If I wasn't anything else, I was a real nigga, and that shit just wasn't flying with me.

Kozlov was sitting at the table talking to man who had his back turned, and when he spotted me coming through the door, a smile appeared on his face.

"My Young Gangsta," Kozlov spoke, and I nodded. "Sit," he instructed."

"Nah, I'm good right here. What's up? What's the meeting about?" I asked.

The nigga turned around, and it was Finesse. I chuckled as I pulled my banger from my waist band and aimed at him.

"Whoa, whoa, Young Gangsta. This is a peace meeting," Kozlov spoke, and again I was confused.

"What the fuck is this about?"

"Well, the girl you were supposed to kill belongs to Finesse, as you know. By you not following through with the hit, it has cost me, you, and even him a lot of money," Kozlov added.

"What the fuck does that mean? Shawty ass ain't got no fucking money." I frowned.

"Nah, but I have a life insurance policy on her. Ten million dollars, and I need to cash in. I owe Mr. Kozlov a lot of money from a gun shipment that got my men locked up. I need to pay my debts." Finesse sounded like a bitch, and I was even more pissed the fuck off.

"You pussy ass nigga, that's yo bitch! You're willing to sacrifice her fucking life for a couple of dollars?"

"No, I'm his bitch." Lanay came from the back room.

I aimed at her and cocked my gun. Finesse hopped up and stood in front of her.

"Please... Geon, like I told you before. I'm sorry," she pleaded

"Y'all muthafuckas set me up back in the day, and now you tryna set up Aspen. Fuck y'all. Y'all lucky Kozlov's men are surrounding this bitch because I would've let loose. But I ain't tryna die today," I said through gritted teeth.

"Kari, go back into the back," Finesse instructed Lanay.

Kari Lanay Hills, the bitch was one of a kind, I can tell you that. And Finesse, whose real name is Lance, was my fucking blood cousin. My mother sent me to live with his mother when I was younger. He was the one who worked in the pawn shop that I had robbed when me and Lanay got pulled over. I shot him to make it believable. If I knew back, then what I know now, I would've killed his disloyal bitch ass.

Imagine my surprise when that nigga left me in jail to fucking rot. He took the money from the heist and started a life in Chicago with it. He didn't visit me, he didn't write, he didn't put money on my books. He said fuck me, and I'll never forget what the fuck he did to me. I didn't know he was in Chicago until Kozlov showed me his picture. I've always had a clue that Lanay was with him but never any evidence. And now here it is, right in my face. The past coming back to haunt me. I guess the only thing I could be grateful for is that the bitch never showed up in court for that fucking kidnapping charge they had on me. I hated both muthafuckas.

"So, I guess ya son ain't really my son, huh? You was fucking my cousin the entire time." I looked at Lanay before she could walk away.

"No... I just needed you to come and see me... so—"

"Hol' up, bruh. She was my bitch before you even came to live with us. We broke up, and then she started fucking with you. But I was smashing her on the regular. So, whatever you thought you had with her was never real. She's always been mine," he stated with a smug look on his face, and I laughed.

"Nigga, I ain't trippin off disloyal pussy. Fuck her," I spat. "Geon... I never meant to hurt you. I—" she tried to explain.

"Go in the fucking back!" Finesse yelled at her, and she scurried away.

Finesse pulled a black duffel bag from underneath the oak table and tried to hand it to me. I knocked the fucking bag outta his hand.

"Fuck is that?" I growled.

"It's your money, cuz. It's your money that I owe you plus interest." He smiled like that shit was gonna make me happy.

"Nigga, fuck that money. I ain't ya fucking cuz! You ain't no fucking family to me! That's chump change to what I'm getting, and I ain't doing shit for you, bitch ass nigga. You lucky I don't find her and tell her what the fuck you plan on doing," I threatened.

"And you will not do that! That's not how I operate business, and you know that! I only asked for this meeting to squash the beef and because you have been paid already, Gangsta."

"I'll give him the money back."

"The client doesn't want it back, they want the job done. So, get the job done! I called on you because I've thought that I could always count on you, but you're slowly proving me wrong, and I don't like to be wrong." Kozlov's voice was stern, and I knew without a doubt that this shit wasn't gonna end well. I couldn't go to war with Kozlov. I wasn't heavy with a team yet.

I weighed my options and exhaled deeply. I felt like a lame ass nigga. Although I didn't wanna harm Aspen, I didn't need a war on my hands either. Fuck, man!

I grabbed the duffel bag that Finesse had dropped, and he stopped me from walking off by grabbing my arm.

"This means our beef is over now, cuz. We were young back then. You gotta let that shit go. It's enough bread in there for you to complete the job."

"Nigga, you fucked my bitch, sent me to prison, and fled town. We gon' always fucking beef. And after I kill yo' bitch, I'm coming back to kill yo' other bitch. You owe me this and her life," I spat at the fuck nigga and walked out of Kozlov's loft.

And now, here we are. I looked at these muthafuckas and knew it was all over for me.

"Where is she?" Kozlov asked me, and I chuckled. "Fuck

you, Kozlov. I thought we were better than that."

"When it comes to money, she'll always have my loyalty. You were disloyal, and this is the price you pay"

"We need that insurance money! Find her!" Lanay screamed at Kozlov's men.

"You don't have to find me, Kari, I'm right here."

Aspen came out of the cut with my AK in her hands, which I forgot I had underneath the bed.

"Why, Finesse?" She looked at him with tears in her eyes, and he sort of hung his head. His coward ass couldn't even answer her.

"Answer me! Why couldn't you do it yourself? Huh?"

"Because I didn't have the heart to, Aspen. Whether you choose to believe it or not, I did love you," Finesse confessed.

"Ah, shut the fuck up!" Lanay screamed as she grabbed the gun from Kozlov's bodyguard and shot Aspen, causing Aspen's finger to hold on to the trigger and let the AK rip.

She was falling and shooting at the same time, and I didn't think she realized it. Kozlov's men, Finesse, and I started to exchange gun fire. I hit Kozlov's guards, two bullets to the dome, and they were down. Kozlov ran out the front door because his old ass wasn't carrying. I kept glancing back at Aspen, and she wasn't moving. I stared at her too long and ended up getting hit in the back of my shoulder blade.

I dropped to the floor and crawled over toward Aspen. Blood flowed from her mouth, and my heart raced.

"G up, baby, don't do this shit. Come on, bae."

I was so focused on her that I forgot about the mayhem around me. "Fall in love in hell, muthafuckas," I heard Finesse say, and the gun

cocked.

"Fuck you, Nig—"
Boom, boom, boom

To be Continued

www.ingramcontent.com/pod-product-compliance
Lightning Source LLC
Chambersburg PA
CBHW021202130726
47988CB00002B/483